THE UNLUCKY

by

Jonas Saul

PUBLISHED BY:

Imagine Press Inc.

Ebook ISBN: 978-1-927404-40-9

Paperback ISBN: 978-1-998047-35-2

Hardcover ISBN: 978-1-998047-36-9

The Unlucky

The Sarah Roberts Series

Dark Visions (One)
The Warning (Two)
The Crypt (Three)
The Hostage (Four)
The Victim (Five)
The Enigma (Six)
The Vigilante (Seven)
The Rogue (Eight)
Killing Sarah (Nine)
The Antagonist (Ten)
The Redeemed (Eleven)
The Haunted (Twelve)
The Unlucky (Thirteen)
The Abandoned (Fourteen)
The Cartel (Fifteen)
Losing Sarah (Sixteen)
The Pact (Seventeen)
The Terror (Eighteen)
The Chase (Nineteen)
The Betrayal (Twenty)
Sarah's Return (Twenty-One)
The Hunt (Twenty-Two)
The Delivery (Twenty-Three)
The Trap (Twenty-Four)
The Ultimatum (Twenty-Five)
The Depraved (Twenty-Six)
The Condemned (Twenty-Seven)
Payback (Twenty-Eight)
The Unknown (Twenty-Nine)
Wrath (Thirty)
The Damned (Thirty-One)
The Game (Thirty-Two)

The Decoy (Thirty-Three)
The Disappearance (Thirty-Four)
The Whole Truth (Thirty-Five)
Alex (Thirty-Six)
Parkman (Thirty-Seven)
Darwin (Thirty-Eight)
Aaron (Thirty-Nine)
Remains To Be Seen (Forty)

The Jake Wood Novels

The Immortal Gene (Book One)
The Immortal Target (Book Two)

Standalone Novels

'Til Death Do Us Part
The Drowning
The Woman in the Woods
The Threat
The Specter
The Mafia Trilogy
A Murder in Time
Frequency of the Dead

Co-Authored Novels

Collision Course (Written with Gary Ponzo)
There Will Be Blood (Written with Rania Stone)
The Soulless (Written with Rania Stone)

Short Story Collections

Twisted Fate (Tales of Horror)

The Unlucky

Twists of Fate (Tales of Hope)

Chapter 1

Everything's cyclical. It all comes back around. From the Earth's rotation to the migration of birds to the lives we live and the habits, we form during those lives. It always comes back around. Everything does. Some call it karma, but that's a dish best served cold and lacking taste. Some call it fate when people imbued with misguided intentions, hurt others and cause destruction in their path. When consequences and accountability must be paid in full, they explain how it was bound to happen that way because you can't escape fate. It seems whether it's pessimism or optimism, it's cyclical.

Sarah Roberts simplified it by accepting things the way they were, forgetting the rest—who needs to carry baggage— and moving on. Do the best you can, have the right intentions, and the inevitability is that everything will work out. If it didn't, then you can smile on your way out of this world, knowing you did your damnedest, your conscience clean. Lady Luck is a fickle bitch. Sometimes she's mingling with others. Hope is all you have when there's nothing else. Removing hope opens a void that only fear can fill. The kind of fear that creeps toward madness. The kind of fear that Sarah might encounter with what she had to do in the next hour.

A strong wind, heated by the summer sun, wailed between the concrete buildings and brushed the hair off Sarah's shoulders as she stared up at the massive CN Tower in downtown Toronto, contemplating fate.

Her eyes glazed over as the wind attempted to dry them. She blinked, collected herself, and stepped forward.

She had been here before. A long time ago. With Drake Bellamy, a man she had saved from a sniper in the Rogers Centre during a baseball game. It was summer, and a ball game was about to get underway. The roof of the huge dome was already open, the sun high, wet spots forming under her arms from the heat.

Or is that my nerves?

Heights were never really an issue for her. It was the fall from those heights that posed a problem. And her dead sister, Vivian, had sent her here to talk to a potential jumper.

She glanced at the ram-air parachute in her hand that cost her nearly fifteen-hundred bucks and shook her head, wondering for the hundredth time why Vivian would want to offer a parachute to someone who was suicidal. But her sister was insistent. There was no other way.

If Sarah learned anything over the past few years, it was to trust Vivian implicitly. Otherwise, people die. That included Sarah, and she didn't want to die today. Her original goal of coming to Toronto was to visit Aaron, her boyfriend. They needed to talk. Deal with whatever was bothering him and see if they could take their relationship to the next step or nowhere at all.

But Vivian had said this side venture wouldn't take long. One quick chat with a potential jumper on the Edgewalk of the CN Tower, and then Sarah could see Aaron soon after.

Sarah put the parachute on like a backpack and started for the ticket booth. She had an hour before the jumper would make a break for the open air, but Sarah wanted to be in place and ready. The extra time allowed her to scout the security, examine the cameras and see how hard it would be to get onto the Edgewalk with a parachute. It was early enough that she could finish this task and still make dinner with Aaron, provided he was available. This was a surprise visit. They hadn't talked since she'd dealt with her abuser, Cole Lincoln, back in Los Angeles. Aaron had a right to move on if that's what he wanted. He just had to do it the right way. The honorable way. He had to explain his intentions to her face, forthright and honest.

With the number of people meandering about, it was a safe assumption that the CN Tower admittance line would be long, but when she got close to the ticket booth, she saw it was relatively short.

She assumed the crowds she walked through to get to the ticket booth were for the baseball game happening next door.

After purchasing the required ticket up the exterior elevator of the tower—and refusing to pay the almost two hundred dollar Edgewalk fee—Sarah got in line to pass through security.

You better be right about this, Vivian.

Sarah's gun was a custom Walther PPK—one of only four hundred made—with a gold eagle on the slide. She had no need of something so special, but it was all she could lay her hands on with such short notice. Its small size made it easy to conceal, and its light weight allowed her to smuggle it into the CN Tower. Vivian had instructed her to seal it in a small lead box and wrap that box in aluminum foil.

People lined up at the machine that puffed air in search of bomb material or residue. When it was her turn, she stepped in, waited the allotted time, and stepped out. No buzzer sounded.

One down, one to go. A clock on the wall said she had forty minutes until the jumper would take a deadly plunge to the concrete below.

She shuffled forward again. The metal detector would be a challenge. There were two security guards, one on either side, motioning people through. She edged closer, ready to explain the inevitable beeping.

The elevator's door yawned open on the other side of the detector, expelling people from the top, waiting to take the next batch up.

Getting through this without raising an alert meant the life or death of the jumper. According to Vivian, it was imperative to make it through.

The first guard, a blond man who had to be in his early twenties, waved for her to enter the detector. The female guard on the other side stepped into Sarah's path with a wand in her hand. She didn't look easily pleased. It seemed something had upset her recently as she gave off an angry aura, her eyes darting left and right like a mouse peeping out of a hole searching for a crazy cat. The guard's bottom lip furrowed in, and she bit down on it.

Habit? Or nerves?

The detector beeped. Sarah stepped out the other side. The female guard motioned for her to raise her arms as Vivian whispered inside Sarah's head.

The guard's nametag read Janet. She bent down, waved the wand along Sarah's left leg, pivoted, and started on her right leg.

"I'm sorry," Sarah whispered.

The guard stopped the wand before it reached Sarah's waist and stood at her full height.

"Did you say something?" Janet asked.

"I said I'm sorry." Sarah leaned closer. "Mike was a prick." She said it just as Vivian instructed. "You deserve better."

Janet blinked and reared back in surprise. She bit down on her lower lip again before asking, "You know Mike?"

"Everything okay?" the blond guard asked from the other side of the detector.

Janet tilted to her right, nodded, and said, "Everything's fine. Just give us a second."

"I've heard of Mike," Sarah added. "And what he did to you."

Janet gave a subtle shake of her head as she struggled to follow.

"It doesn't matter," Sarah said. "It's still shitty to do what he did and then text you about it."

Janet's eyes filled with tears at the mention of the text. Water collected on her lower lids, bulged, then spilled over and down her cheeks.

"I only got the text an hour ago," Janet said. "How could

you already know …"

"Word travels fast. Hey, I just wanted to say I was sorry to hear what happened. Sister to sister."

The wand, completely forgotten, Janet set it aside, produced a Kleenex from her uniform pocket, wiped her eyes, and blew her nose.

"Look," Sarah said. "I'm meeting friends topside for a bite to eat in the restaurant. We cool?"

"You okay?" the other guard asked again. "Getting a bit of a line back here."

"We're good," Janet said, a nasal sound to her voice as it filled with emotion drawn by the tears.

Sarah started for the elevator, not believing her luck. She had a metal clip for a wallet, a metal belt buckle to deflect from the gun's box, and aluminum foil shoved into the bottom of the backpack parachute. Worst case, she would draw the weapon, get upstairs and lock the floor down, thereby stopping the jumper. But doing this quietly would be better for Sarah and less embarrassing for the jumper.

"Hey!" Janet called after her.

Sarah turned around just short of the elevator.

"Thanks. Just a heads up. Don't order the butternut squash bisque or the cauliflower soup. Bit nasty. The rest of the menu is cool, but not those two."

The elevator door opened. Sarah nodded and mouthed the word *thanks* as people filed out.

Three people who had left her through the metal detector stepped onto the elevator. Sarah followed. The doors closed, and Sarah exhaled a sigh of relief as the lift headed up.

Before seeing Aaron, Vivian had said this jaunt wouldn't take long, and it was easy. Come prepared, and everything will work out. She would even get her through security because causing a scene and forcing her way through would have created questions that needed answering and delays she wasn't interested in taking.

But how did you know talking about some guy named Mike would set her off and let me walk right through? Their security seems a little lax here.

On the ascent up the exterior side of the tower, Vivian explained that Janet would quit her job by Friday. Mike was her supervisor. They'd had an affair. Mike was supposed to leave his wife. He hadn't. An hour before Sarah walked through the metal detector, Janet had heard that she was the fourth employee to have an affair with Mike within the past six months. He was a serial cheater, and Janet had been mistakenly convinced they would get married one day. She didn't care about her job, and when Sarah offered kindness, Janet passed her through without another thought, like an employee stealing from the till of a store because they feel a sense of entitlement. Letting Sarah through without doing a thorough job was Janet's version of rebelling. Janet had silently wished Sarah to come today with devious intent as the elevator door closed. Maybe it would teach Mike to be a better person.

Near the top of the tower, Sarah stared out the window at the hot concrete surface of Toronto—the elevated highways, the busy people running around the base of the skyscrapers, and the lake off to her left. The Rogers Centre almost appeared attached to the CN Tower from this height. Its roof was indeed open. Inside, men in blue uniforms scurried around the baseball diamond as the crowd of thousands cheered, a din barely audible over the elevator noise. Before the elevator entered an enclosure and the outside disappeared, she thought of Drake, dead now for quite some time, and how she had connected with him instantly.

Could there have been anything serious with Drake? She thought not. Aaron had her heart. She belonged to him. All she had to do was let him know so he could stop fucking around and get with the program.

The doors opened behind her. She turned and followed the people out, taking in her surroundings. She knew the jumper was female, early twenties. All Vivian told her was to be at the entrance to the Edgewalk by 2:17 p.m. She would have to convince whoever was at the door to let her out to talk to the jumper. It was the only way. She was to bring the Walther PPK as well, but so far, Sarah had no idea why a gun would be needed to stop a suicide.

She headed for the nearest restroom, pushed past two teenage girls with too much makeup, and found an empty stall near the back wall. Once inside, she pulled out the metal box and unwrapped the Walther PPK. After sliding it into the back of her jeans, she balled the tin foil up and tossed it in the trash dispenser. She placed the small metal box back inside the pocket of the ram-air parachute pack.

After that, Sarah headed back out, using a paper towel on the door handle, and walked around the tower in search of the Edgewalk entrance. Two p.m. She was ready for whatever was going to happen with time to spare.

Families had come to make a day of it. Children huddled close to their parents as they all stared down at the city far below. A couple of kids acted up, the unruly result of lazy parenting. A family of four with British accents passed by, each clutching an ice cream, chocolate for the small boy.

Thoughts of children passed through Sarah's mind. What would it be like to have children? It wasn't the first time she had thought of kids. But raising them in this world, the one she had gotten to know over the past few years, scared her. She had seen enough death, degradation, and pain to last more than a lifetime. Crime statistics, rogue cops, illegal shootings, terrorist bombings, wars—all this information was out there for anyone who wanted to find it. The daily news covered everything, and yet women still had babies, day after day, in the thousands, all over the planet.

Sarah moved on, circling the tower, knowing in the midst of all the carnage she had seen and will see, she too would have a baby one day. She not only hoped Aaron was there to see that day, but she also hoped he would be the father.

Two security guards trudged by, busy watching the tourists until one nudged the other and leaned in to whisper something in his ear. Sarah caught what their eyes had found. An attractive woman in a red blouse and short skirt leaned over the railing by the window to catch a better look down. Her skirt had risen, exposing most of her long legs. The guards had slowed to wait and see if the skirt would continue upward.

The name *Mike* echoed through Sarah's mind, subtle and smooth like smoke passing over velvet.

She changed course and approached the woman who hadn't noticed the men gawking.

"You're offering front-row seats to those guys," Sarah whispered.

The woman didn't move at first. Then she lowered her upper body more, exposing the hem of her lace panties.

Sarah frowned. *What the hell?*

"Maybe I want the attention," the woman said, her voice deep and masculine.

Transvestite?

Before the woman turned and gazed upon Sarah, it all came together. It was a man standing beside her, dressed as a woman. He wore lipstick, mascara, a blond wig, and an expression of sheer joy at the drawing of men's eyes.

"To each their own." Sarah backed away, a *hmmph* escaping her lips.

The Edgewalk entrance came up on her right. She went to the observation window and watched the people outside on the edge. They were dressed in red suits and tied to a rope that tethered them to a bar-like structure above their heads. Their arms were thrust out like wings while they leaned over the edge.

You'd never catch me doing that.

When buying the ram-air parachute, she had looked up B.A.S.E. jumping and discovered that anything less than about 2,000 feet needed a static line, a line that pulled the chute out at the instant the jumper took air. The CN Tower was just over 1,800 feet high. She hoped whoever she gave the chute to could survive with the two-hundred-foot deficit.

Five minutes to spare.

The Edgewalkers were heading back to the door, their session ending. Sarah pivoted slowly on her heels and took in the crowd. The two guards had finished gawking at the ladyboy and stood near the door as the walkers returned to safety and were unhooked from their tethers.

The crowd had thinned, but no one stood out. No single female appeared desperate. No one crying. Nothing that made anyone look suicidal. But what did suicidal look like anyway?

CCTV cameras were everywhere, filming everything. They had recorded Sarah in several places. They would have clear images of her face. The Toronto police had worked with Sarah several times in the past. It wouldn't take more than an hour for everyone to know who she was if they needed an identity.

Once she talked the jumper back off the edge or made her take the backpack parachute, she would be revered, so there'd be no need for cameras and identity searches. Otherwise, she would've worn a disguise.

One more look at Mike, the dog that he was, made her want to hurt him. When Sarah talked to Janet downstairs, she felt her pain for a moment. Aaron had left Sarah in California. It was the first time a man in her life had walked away. Drake was her first love interest, but he'd never walked away. He was murdered. Aaron was her man. Walking away like that hurt. She would've denied those feelings years ago, but now it mattered. Closure mattered. And people like Janet mattered. Mike needed to know that.

Sarah slipped by two men standing near the window and moved closer to the entrance of the Edgewalk.

2:15 p.m.

After one more slow, careful look around for a suicidal jumper, Sarah slipped the ram-air parachute off her back and held it in her left hand, keeping her right available for the Walther PPK if she needed it.

2:16 p.m.

She saw her. Brunette. Olive skinned. Prominent nose, intense eyes. Gorgeous girl. Long flowing hair. Possible Italian heritage. The suicidal look was in her eyes—the intensity, the fear didn't fit for a tour of the CN Tower. Her brown shirt opened in a V, exposing the white of her bra and the purple of a bruise near her neckline. She wore yoga pants that left nothing to the imagination. Without having to glance over to confirm it, Sarah knew Mike would be checking this girl out, and that was the last thing she needed.

As she neared Sarah's position, the girl brought her hands together and typed furiously on a cell phone. The time on the clock to Sarah's right confirmed it was as Vivian had predicted. Maybe she could pull the girl aside and talk to her before she made a scene.

But that option died instantly as the girl darted for the open door. Mike was about to shut it. She jammed her forearm inside just in time and yelped as the door closed on it.

"Hey!" Mike exclaimed.

Sarah jumped into action but was too late.

Mike went to say something else, but the girl raised her hand and jabbed the base of her palm toward Mike's face, shutting down any further argument from him. He stumbled back, released the door, and grabbed at his bloody mouth.

The jumper yanked the door open and stepped out onto the platform with no form of protection—no ropes, no tethers. She staggered on her feet for a moment in the wind, dipped her head, and moved away from the door toward the edge.

Sarah got to the door, but before opening it to go after the jumper, she dropped the ram-air backpack low and swung it into Mike's unsuspecting face. It smacked his hand into his injured mouth. He groaned and squealed under his breath. The other guard had moved away as he talked on his radio.

"Stop fucking around at work," Sarah said. "Now your wife will hear about it, and Janet's pissed. Not to mention the other girls you've been sleeping with. Best you quit your job and leave town, asshole."

Sarah slipped through the door and pulled it closed behind her.

The jumper snapped her head around to see who had followed her out. She raised her hands to ward Sarah off, a pained, frantic expression on her face.

"Stay where you are, or I'll jump," she yelled, her voice almost swallowed by the wind.

Sarah took a moment to collect herself by lowering her center of gravity as the wind buffeted from all sides. The height was unimaginable.

To focus on the jumper was to stop from falling. To not focus on the jumper was to experience vertigo, spin around, and be lost in the air.

She thought she had prepared for this, but nothing prepared her for the abyss to her right. She could almost feel the Grim Reaper in the area, waiting for the soul of the one who fell. The one who swooned and fainted lost over the edge because of an extra strong wind or light-headedness at the immensity of the height.

She set the parachute by her feet, raised a hand to not alarm the jumper, and got down on one knee. It may have appeared calming to the jumper—a non-threatening posture —but it was more to gather herself.

"It's okay," Sarah said loud enough to be heard over the wind. "I'm here to talk."

"There's nothing to talk about. I have to die. That's all there is to it."

"No. You don't. No one has to die."

Famous last words, Vivian whispered inside Sarah's head.

What does that mean? Sarah asked, but Vivian quieted.

The girl's gaze shifted toward Sarah with those intense eyes, her hair billowing up behind her head with the wind. "I do. I have to die."

"Tell me why, then," Sarah said. "Why do you have to die?"

"No," the girl shouted. "Because if you found out what's going on, you'd want to die, too."

"What could be so wrong that you have to *die*?" Sarah adjusted to her other knee. The wind calmed for a moment. To her left, the window was smeared with the faces of people as if they were spread on the viewing glass with a butter knife. Random flashes of cameras blinked as people took photos and filmed what they thought was about to be a suicide. Sarah idly wondered how long before this was on YouTube.

When she had glanced away, the girl moved closer to the edge. One strong wind from behind could easily send this girl tumbling to certain death; she was that close to the edge now.

"Let's talk," Sarah shouted. "I can help."

"How?" the girl yelled back, her words laced with what sounded like anger. "How can you help? I don't know you. These people are too powerful. They're hidden underground. There's nothing anyone can do. I'm finished. I'm used up. I'm done. I can't face my father, and I won't go on living like this anymore. They have left me no options."

Tears filled her eyes. The girl dropped to her knees, and for that brief instant, Sarah was sure she was going over the edge.

"Wait!" someone yelled from behind them.

Sarah spun around. Two armed guards had opened the door and stepped out behind her.

"Ma'am, please step back from the ledge."

"Fuck you!" the girl shouted, then moved so close that her knees cleared the edge. All she had to do was lean forward now. There was nothing stopping her. "Get back, or I'm gone."

Sarah waved frantically for them to retreat. They hesitated.

"Go!" she shouted. When they hesitated again, she drew her weapon, aimed it slightly left, away from their faces and the people inside, and fired. The report was loud but muffled by the noise of the wind, the message clear. The door slammed shut, and even over the wind, she heard the lock engage.

The jumper hadn't moved. But now she was crying, her upper body shaking with sobs.

"I can help," Sarah said. At a loss for words, she couldn't think of anything else to say. Vivian hadn't explained why this girl was supposed to be talked down. All Sarah knew was to be there on time and to bring the parachute and the gun.

"You can't help. It all ends in death, and I refuse to be cremated."

Sarah frowned. *Cremated?*

"Here, take this," Sarah said. She held out the parachute. "Jump then, but take this."

"I came to die, not jump with a parachute."

Something caught Sarah's eye on the wall to the left of the girl. A large red sign advertised what the Edgewalk participants were experiencing. It depicted a large photo of the CN Tower and its total height of 553 meters, just over 1,800 feet. A red dot the size of a golf ball coupled with a red arrow said *You Are Here.* It was clearly marked as the rim where the Edgewalk took place, and the height was written in big, bold letters as 356 meters.

That left the Edgewalk eight hundred feet short of the recommended 2,000 feet for a jump with this kind of parachute, minus the static line. The parachute would have to be already open at this height. Sarah wasn't a skydiver, but from her brief research, it was dicey for a B.A.S.E. jumper to make it without a static line from this height. Or they'd at least have a nasty landing. Although she surmised it would probably be better to have a parachute than not have one at all.

The girl swung her legs over the edge and dangled them, her hands on her thighs. It appeared she was examining where she would land over a thousand feet below.

Through the wind and the sounds of the city, the distinct wail of sirens made its way to Sarah. The police were here, and there would be more on their way. Now she would have to explain how she got a gun past security. She would probably get that security guard Janet in trouble as cameras would pick up how she let Sarah in even after the metal detector beeped.

But all that could be handled later.

"There has to be something I can do," Sarah said. "Is there anything you want?"

The girl made eye contact with Sarah.

"All I want is to die, to finish this. Then the raping will stop. The torture, humiliation, degradation, and constant flow of men will stop. Death will set me free. It all ends with death. I refuse to be cremated. My suicide will spark an investigation. Maybe someone will find out what's been happening. Maybe my death will help others escape these people—"

"Tell me about it. I can help you." Sarah moved closer, parachute in one hand, gun in the other. "Let's get to the bottom of this together."

The girl sawed a wrist across her eyes, wiping them. "You don't understand. This life isn't for me. I *want* to die. I've made my decision. I'm already dead on the inside. All I'm doing is killing the outside. Then no one can have me anymore. I'll be free."

Sarah moved closer still. Peripheral vision offered movement at the windows as cops filled the observation area, displacing the gawkers. The moment was upon them. The girl was going over if Sarah didn't do something within a few seconds, but she was still too far away to grab the girl's arm.

Literally, this was a do-or-die moment.

The wind abated. She had broken out in a full-body sweat. Eight feet in front of her, the girl looked as if she sat on a dock overlooking a lake, dangling her feet in the water, bent forward in an attempt to locate fish or stare at her reflection. This was lunacy.

"Please, don't," Sarah said. "It's not worth it." The girl didn't acknowledge her. "At least take this, then. Strap it on. Pull the cord and jump. It'll give you a chance."

"I don't want a chance. If I live after this, they will hunt me down and kill me. But not before tying me to a bed for six months and having every ape of a man do whatever he wishes to me. I'm ruined. It's okay. I accept that now and take back the power over my own life." She turned to Sarah. "Why can't you accept it?" She scooted her buttocks closer to the edge. "Sometimes death is the right answer."

The realization of what was happening struck Sarah like marbles in a sock hitting her in the temple. She stumbled on her knee and tilted toward the edge.

She wasn't supposed to save this girl. She was supposed to meet her, hear her out. Nothing could save this girl. Her mind was made up, and Vivian knew this.

The access door opened behind Sarah. The cops probably figured out Sarah wasn't doing a good job of negotiating the girl back from the edge.

The girl looked past Sarah's shoulder. "I told you to stay inside. Now I have to jump."

Sarah's hand numbed. *Vivian?*

Her arm numbed.

A blackout? Now?

Then Vivian took over her gun hand. She raised it against Sarah's will. Inside Sarah, there was no conflict. Whenever Vivian took over, it was Vivian knows best. Her insight far exceeded anything Sarah could grasp or possibly know at any given moment.

"Stop!" was all Sarah could think of saying as the Walther PPK was aimed at the girl's head.

When Sarah comprehended what Vivian was doing, she tried to fight her sister's control over her body, but to no avail.

"Freeze!" a man yelled behind her.

The girl was smiling so wide, her bloodshot eyes slitted, and the whites of her teeth jutted between her lips. She truly was at peace. She had made it, and it was on her own terms.

The jumper tilted at a forty-five-degree angle. One second she was sitting on the edge; the next, she had gone too far to recover. In that brief moment, Vivian repeatedly applied pressure to the trigger of the Walther PPK.

The word *No!* shot through Sarah's mind as the gun fired against Sarah's will. Before the girl disappeared completely over the edge and out of sight, bullets entered her chest and neck.

Then the girl was gone, along with the fine misty spray of blood from Sarah's bullets.

Movement at the window stopped. Everyone was frozen in a gasp of shock. This would go down as a murder in cold blood, even though the girl would've died anyway. Cameras recorded it. This wasn't a suicide, after all. For whatever reason—and only Vivian knew that at the moment—the girl needed to be murdered. That was why she got Sarah to buy the ram-air parachute.

It was not to save the jumper. It was for Sarah's escape.

Oh no, she thought. *Fuck my life.*

As Vivian relinquished her arm and Sarah regained control, the Walther PPK slipped from her grasp. She swung the parachute around her back and jammed her hands through the straps. How could she not see this before? You talk jumpers off ledges. You don't offer them a parachute, a free, safe ride to the bottom. They wanted to die, not *risk* their life.

Instead of getting up and offering a larger target for the police, their guns already out, Sarah whispered a silent prayer to God, cursed Vivian for fucking with her, and rolled over the edge of the CN Tower, pushing with her legs away from the building to avoid bumping into it on the way down, instantly gaining intense speed.

Within a second of open air, she yanked the rip cord and hoped it was enough.

The wind whipped her face back, and without goggles, her eyes watered almost to the point of blindness. She wiped at them in an attempt to see where the hell she was headed. When the chute opened, it drew back on her arms and stomach. The ground was still so far away that she imagined herself vomiting and wondered if it would beat her to the ground.

The wind buffeted her, forcing her toward Lake Ontario as the falling sensation in her stomach eased. It was like the world's most insane roller coaster with no track and no secure car to sit in, just open air and a wish and a prayer.

She glanced up at the rectangular chute to reassure herself it was open and working. Two toggles dangled on either side of her. She grabbed them and attempted to steer right, then left. It worked to a certain degree.

With one look over her shoulder, she saw the elevator heading up the side of the CN Tower. It was packed with at least ten people, all in police uniforms. Even from this distance, she could tell their eyes were on her.

She turned back and concentrated on making a safe landing somewhere. She would need to exit the area fast, get somewhere safe, and find out what Vivian was up to.

A huge green landing strip looked like the best possible solution—the baseball diamond where the Blue Jays played a home game. She steered that way as the dome of the Rogers Centre was coming up fast. Already people in the audience were looking up at her descent, pointing skyward.

A moment later, she cleared the edge of the open roof, steering for a perfect shot down the middle of the field. But she was too high, coming down toward the bleachers at the back. There would be no place to have a running landing.

She yanked on the left toggle. It nearly flipped the parachute upside down, tossing her sideways. She released it and pulled easier on the right one. It straightened her out as she flew over second base, heading toward the outfield.

To her left, the gigantic Sony Jumbotron picked her up, and the crowd went wild.

She tugged on both toggles at the same time just before smashing into the ground. Then she was running, the ground coming too fast. She hit it hard, smacked a knee, dropped onto her right shoulder, and rolled, the lines of the parachute wrapping around her.

The crowd cheered her insane landing, the raucous noise energizing her as she pulled herself out of the chute, untangled her legs, and got to her feet, pushing the rest of the chute away from her.

Just like the day she ran out of the Rogers Centre with Drake Bellamy, she stood ten feet from the exit they had used. Baseball players and Toronto police were running across the field toward her.

She took off at a fast clip, made an exit in seconds flat, disappeared around a corner, hit a door to the outside, and ran into traffic, where she hopped into a waiting taxi.

"Hundred bucks to get me away from my controlling boyfriend. Go now!"

The driver dropped the car in gear and left rubber on the pavement as he peeled out.

It wasn't for at least two blocks before she started breathing normally again.

Then Vivian started talking …

Chapter 2

THE MINISTER HELD THE Bible in one hand as he read from it. The words drifted and rolled with the soft summer breeze, falling on the ears of the mourners. Some cried. Others held strong in their vigil of grief as they stared at the wooden coffin, a single rose resting atop.

Timothy Simmons held his composure and waited for the funeral of his daughter to finish. Under other circumstances, he would have appreciated the others that showed up to honor her. He would have been more gracious to them, more open. But grieving the only daughter he ever had, and at such a young age, muddied his social abilities. He had muttered his thanks, nodded his awareness of what was happening, and spent the rest of the funeral acting the part of a dazed zombie who might be mingling through the crowd trying to decide which brain to chew.

As a cop on the Toronto police force going on twenty

years—now a detective—Tim had seen a lot of death, even caused a few. But the death of his only daughter—and by gunshot—brought him to a place of anger where only retribution could ease his suffering or offer closure. Friends and family whispering to one another, stealing glances his way, thought they saw sadness and grief on his features, but they didn't. The tears were fury, and the tight jaw, locked features, and stern expression were one of absolute aggression. He would find the woman who did this. He had been a detective long enough to find her quickly. He would learn what motivated her to shoot his only daughter, and then he would drive her to his associates at the warehouse, where they would ruin her without killing her, leaving that pleasure for him.

Since the victim was his daughter, he had been blocked from the investigation. Niles Mason and Marina Diner, two stellar detectives, had been assigned to locate the girl who shot his daughter on the Edgewalk of the CN Tower and then jumped to escape the authorities.

Niles might offer Tim inside information on how the case was going, but not Marina. Marina had the lead on the case, and nobody got any information out of her unless Marina deemed it public knowledge.

Tim was okay with that. Marina had a process; if anybody respected that process, that was fellow detective Timothy Simmons. But when someone executes the daughter of a cop, the rules go out the window. All cops knew that. Tim may not be involved with the investigation directly, but he should at least be informed of its progress without resorting to methods of subterfuge to access information unless the detective in charge was Marina Diner.

It didn't help that Tim's left hand was newly broken. When he heard what had happened to Vanessa, he exploded with rage at the people he thought had ordered her murder. His associates were vile and brutal, but would they order the death of his daughter when he was someone of such value to them?

Tim refused to believe it. He couldn't understand it. He had raged against the thought, punching the kitchen cupboards after they'd visited to inform him about Vanessa. The thin veneer of his cupboards broke after the third slug, and his left hand pushed through, the knuckles making contact with the flat side of the shelf that held coffee cups, snapping the index finger and middle finger bones. The pain did nothing to soothe his temper or anger. If anything, he held the people responsible for his daughter's death accountable for the broken hand.

His associates had been quiet for the past three days leading up to the funeral, effectively going underground. The investigation had been shrouded in secrecy, and Tim had learned nothing about the shooter except what the papers reported. A lone female, blond, maybe a hundred-twenty pounds, sopping wet, with long hair, and extremely fit. The security cameras were pulled, and the witnesses were commandeered and interviewed in secrecy. Only a photo or two had made it to the newspapers, and one shaky, grainy video hit YouTube. There was no way to make a positive ID from the information he had.

So he let it go for now. He would handle the funeral. Bury his daughter. Then find the murderer and the reason. He'd push for answers. Call in favors. Worst case, he would expose the consortium, the associates he feared, for what it was and probably die in the process or be imprisoned for his involvement, but letting a murderer walk was unconscionable. And Tim knew that the woman who pulled the trigger wasn't the only murderer. The people behind her were involved, and there was no way he would let any of them walk from this without paying what they owed. Everyone always had to pay what they owed. That was his mantra as a cop, and it stayed with him as a detective. Cause and effect. Yin and yang. Karma. Didn't matter what anyone called it, it all came back to accountability, and everyone had to pay what they owed. That was all there was to it.

He shuffled from one foot to the other, a line of sweat sliding down his spine. Could the female shooter be an assassin or a hired gun, or was this a random event? How did the shooter get a gun and a parachute past security and up to the top of the CN Tower? Someone had answers, and someone had to be held responsible.

He was sure this had something to do with the consortium that protected his associates. Suicide could be explained away. But murdering Vanessa brought heat. What they didn't expect was the kind of heat Timothy would bring.

The minister broke through Tim's reverie as he snapped the Bible closed and stepped back. Someone's hand gently tapped Tim's shoulder. Another hand squeezed his triceps. People stepped away as the coffin was lowered to the ground. Tim moved to the side, burrowed his hand into the dirt, and tossed a small clump on the plush-lined vessel that contained his daughter.

It sank lower, moving away from him. When it stopped at the bottom, he gazed around at the attendees all dressed in black. People lined up to offer condolences and soft words of grief. Some shook his hand, while others pumped it. He accepted each gesture while staring into their eyes. Certain killers visit the funerals of their victims. Members of the consortium were here. Which one was privy to details? What person among the mourners knew more than they let on? He trusted no one and suspected everyone. Until the people responsible for Vanessa's death were rooted out and dealt with as the filth they were, he wouldn't rest. And even then, could he ever be how he was before this tragic event? Losing a child changes something fundamental inside a parent. He felt that change and embraced it. Welcomed it now that he had no choice. That change propelled him forward in the face of loss and sadness. It made him hungry for the truth at all costs. Whether he lost his job, career, or life didn't matter anymore as he had lost his one true joy—his daughter.

All that mattered now was collecting what was owed.

He shook one last hand as the mourners slipped away silently and trudged across the well-kept lawn of the cemetery. He lingered by the hole in the ground, his daughter's body at the bottom. The sky was cloudless, not a blemish to be seen. The air smelled of pine needles and freshly cut grass. It took him back to the summer when he met his wife. The summer of love, they once called it. Carefree, young, at the start of their lives, ready to take on the world.

Then she got pregnant.

Vanessa was on her way, and eighteen years ago, in March, she was born, killing her mother in the process, giving Tim only three short years with the woman of his dreams.

It ruined him for women after that. He raised Vanessa as

best he could, never blaming her for the death of his wife, not even subconsciously. He made sure to do right by Vanessa, to lead by example, and raise her to be the woman his wife would be proud of. He made mistakes along the way, but who didn't? Overall, Vanessa was the apple of his eye, the love of his life, and the life jacket in the ocean of crime he always drowned in. Her love kept him afloat when the world threatened to take him down.

But now she was dead. She was gone. That left him alone in the vast ocean, preparing to go under. Yet there was something comforting about that. He was in a unique position to bring down a lot of people with him.

He pulled his sunglasses from atop his head over his eyes and scanned the area. Most of the mourners had left. He had detected nothing untoward from them. As far as he could tell, no one seemed to be spying on the funeral from a distance. Who could keep an eye on the event with Marina Diner here? She had a small team of officers acting like sentries, watching, and guarding the area. No one could have been observing his daughter's funeral unless from far away with a high-powered telescope.

Marina Diner leaned against his car, waiting for him. Without hope of getting any information out of her and unwilling to offer any himself, Tim started for his car.

She watched as he traversed the gravestones, stepping over flat ones and meandering around tall ones. He felt her eyes on him and could almost taste her self-righteousness. She was one of the few on the force who drove the rest of them mad with her military discipline and dogged determination to cross every T and dot every I. The do-gooder. The goody two shoes. Adam Ant once belted out a song about her.

"Detective Diner," Tim addressed her as he approached. "You're not all in black."

"Black pants and jacket," she replied, not a hint of a smile or a pleasing gesture on her face.

"White shirt." Tim stopped short of her. He avoided her eyes. If she could see past the shaded lens of his sunglasses, he didn't want her to see what was in his. She was good at figuring people out. She was one of the best detectives on the force.

"You doing okay?" she asked.

"What do you think?"

A silence descended between them. Tim shuffled his feet and kicked at a pebble. He waited for her to state why she came. After a moment, she pushed off the car and stepped closer.

Her hand dropped on his shoulder. "Sorry to hear you broke your hand."

He blinked and pulled his head back in surprise.

"What?" Marina asked. "Why the surprised look, Tim?"

"The hand? My broken hand? Really? That's why you're sorry?"

"Yeah, you broke it. Must've hurt like a bitch."

Why no mention of Vanessa? Where's the *I'm sorry about your loss*? Or the proverbial, *my condolences*? Did she know something he didn't? How many cops were involved with the consortium that protected his associates? Did any of them know of his involvement? Or was she pushing, prodding, waiting for a crack to appear? Was she trying to trip him up or wind him up?

"Whatever," Tim mumbled under his breath. He

shambled away, her hand dropping from his shoulder.

"Tim?"

He grasped the door handle and looked up. Her face was shrouded in the light of the falling sun. Even with sunglasses, he had to look away.

"We'll find who did this," she said.

"I know."

"*I'll* find who did this."

He raised a hand to ward off the sun. "Not if I find them first." He dropped into the car and slammed the door.

After a pause, she headed to her own car, an unmarked cruiser, and got in. He waited until her vehicle disappeared down the lane before he allowed the tears. He wept in silence, alone, thoughts of Vanessa growing up, her dreams of being in show business, and lately her teenage angst. He'd do anything to have her beside him. Anything. But even he had to pay what was due, and someone thought he owed a lot.

That someone thought wrong.

A car approached from the same lane that Marina had just disappeared down. As the white Dodge Charger eased up beside him, a lone female driving, he opened the center console and wrapped his fingers around the handle of his gun. Weapon in hand, he studied the driver's face as the vehicle slowed. He couldn't escape the fact that she resembled a girl he thought was dead. Some Eastern European girl he met once at a meeting. An Elizabeth, or Erzabet, or something Eastern European bloc sounding. She had Laura Ingalls braids like on *Little House on the Prairie*. The kind that is somewhat out of fashion but comes back occasionally.

She hadn't looked at him yet as her window eased down. He wiped at his face to clear the moisture from his cheeks, then pushed the window button on the car door with the baby finger of his broken left hand. His right hand squeezed the butt of the gun still hidden in the console between the seats, his palm sweaty, the handle slipping a bit.

It had been widely reported that a lone female in her mid-twenties, with long hair, and in shape, had shot his daughter. Who was to say this wasn't the same girl?

"I can help," the girl said, her face aimed straight ahead, features unmoving. She still hadn't glanced his way.

His gut instinct triggered a warning as adrenaline filled his stomach. Something about this woman's calm, austere manner warned him to be cautious around her.

He eased the gun from the console and placed it on his lap.

"Who are you?" he asked. "And how can you help *me*?" Whoever she was, this woman had bad timing, and if she really wanted to help, why wait until the funeral, four days since Vanessa had been shot, to approach him?

Slowly, with countless years of practice, he thumbed the safety off and brought the weapon into firing position just below the edge of the door. One sudden move and an extremely fast bullet would enter this braided girl's head near the temple. Or maybe he would go for the cheek. Better yet, the throat. Yeah, a bullet to the throat for his daughter's murderer.

"I know who ordered the kill," the girl said.

That stunned him. He reared back a notch, the gun dipping until it rested on his left thigh.

"Who?" escaped his lips, almost as if he croaked the

word from the back of his throat.

"Not here. They're probably watching."

It was maddening how she stared straight ahead, unmoving except for her lips, and barely at that. She was so stock-still that images of a Roman statue popped into his head from the time he vacationed in Rome.

"Then where?"

"The Office."

"What? My office?"

"No, *The* Office. The restaurant on John Street where you used to go for Tuesday night wings in the nineties with your fellow officers. Before you made detective."

Stunned again, his eyes widened, and his mouth hung open. A subtle shake of his head dislodged the sludge in his thinking. He gathered himself, the grip on the handle of the service weapon tightening, his palm slick with moisture.

"What are you, twenty-two years old? How would someone so young know that about me?"

"I know more than I want to know."

"Who are you?" he asked again, this time with more pleading in his voice.

"My name is Erzabet. We almost met once before. You may remember me from a party."

This had to be a cruel joke. Her words were spoken as if she could read his mind from moments before.

"You don't have an accent."

"I lost it."

He stared at her profile longer, taking her in, considering his options. If she was serious, then he had to hear her out. If she were the murderer, then he would have to take her out. If he failed, at least he had a face and a name, providing it really was her name.

"When?" he asked.

"Now."

He shrugged. "Why not."

"Follow me." Her engine revved, and she sped away.

He tossed the gun into the passenger seat and waited until she performed a U-turn behind him, watching her every move in the mirror. Then she passed his vehicle heading the way Marina had gone only ten minutes before.

After checking his mirrors and seeing no one, he followed the strange girl in braids. She sped up on the open road, but he stayed close.

He considered calling this in, just in case. Maybe having a cop at the restaurant in another booth would help if this Erzabet was psychotic. But the nature of the information could compromise him with the consortium.

No, he had to do this alone, and damn the consequences. He would hear her out and decide what to do next.

It was moments like these that he wished he hadn't broken his hand. He might need it. If she turned out to be his daughter's murderer, then killing her in a restaurant was out of the question. Kidnapping her and dragging her body to an abandoned building or a dump site would be taxing with one hand.

None of that mattered, though. What were the odds that the murderer would approach him at the funeral and offer help? That was utterly insane. And how could she know what he did over fifteen years ago? She would have been ten years old then.

At worst, she knew someone who knew a lot about him and that someone had a message for him. At best, that message would aid in apprehending Vanessa's murderer.

And Timothy Simmons intended to hear that message because everyone had to pay what was due.

Eventually, every debt came due; some just had more interest tacked on than others.

Compound interest.

Chapter 3

THE OFFICE HAD CHANGED a lot since he was here last. He had heard it was renovated recently and was often confused with the one that used to be in another part of Toronto called Etobicoke. But he hadn't been inside it in over seven years. Long time considering it was one of his drinking spots every week back in the day.

He had stayed on the Charger's tail quite well, having been with the force for twenty years. Following people was one of the job descriptions. Add to that knowledge of the streets of Toronto, equal or better than any taxi driver, and you've got a tail that's hard to slip.

He had recorded the Charger's license plate number. Even considered calling it in on his cell phone as he wasn't in his unmarked cruiser and didn't have access to his police computer and database. The problem, though, was it would link back to him if he had to shoot the girl. So he recorded the license number in case she got away. At least then, they'd know who they were looking for.

It was probably a rented car. Enterprise Rent-A-Car brought in Dodge Chargers. In his job, it was good to stay on top of what agency rented what makes and models of cars. The woman probably used a fake name and ID if it was a rental.

Again, he concluded that it was best to hear her out and then decide what to do.

The woman angled into a spot in front of Hooters, the restaurant across from The Office. He drove past her and turned into an underground parking garage. Once he had parked and turned off the car, he secured his service weapon in the console, popped the trunk, and got out.

He glanced around to ensure no one was close enough to see what he was doing, then opened the spare tire cover and retrieved a small metal box. From it, he withdrew a tiny, unregistered handgun. The serial number had been shaved off by a punk he busted down in the Beaches area for petty theft a few years back. The asshole was so high he didn't even know if he had a gun on him or not. When he sobered up, the perp was smart enough to not bring up the subject of the weapon to avoid incriminating himself.

After checking to ensure it was loaded and ready to be used, Tim slipped it into his suit jacket pocket. Then he slammed the trunk and started for the street.

No one followed them on the drive from the cemetery, and he couldn't see anyone lingering in a car or watching his approach from behind a tree or the corner of a building.

The Charger hadn't moved. He knew the risk he took by entering the parking garage, momentarily being out of sight.

But the girl wouldn't have approached him at the funeral, driven this far, and then taken off when he wasn't looking. No, this meeting was about to take place, and he suspected he would learn something he wasn't sure he was ready to hear. But, like a lemming staring over the edge, he knew he would jump—with both feet.

Nothing less for Vanessa.

Nothing less.

He opened the door of The Office Pub and entered.

Chapter 4

Aaron Stevens stretched his arms on his apartment's balcony, yawning and moaning. It had been another long night of worry.

Where was Sarah?

He had thought this was over for him. He loved her deeply. But being with someone who was kidnapped, shot at, and constantly on the edge of death had become a bit overwhelming. Sarah had painted a permanent bull's eye on her forehead by willingly leading the life she led, and she wasn't prepared to wash it off.

In California, Aaron had broken down. Ashamed to admit it, ashamed to face her, he'd left California and returned to Toronto. Previously, he planned to take a break to focus on his dojo business. They had agreed that he would go back to teaching Shotokan karate. He needed to give his overworked instructors time off. Sarah had understood and actually pushed him to go.

But leaving when Cole Lincoln had kidnaped her was probably bad timing.

Didn't she always prevail, though?

Dressed only in track pants, he stretched again, anticipating his hour-long yoga session, and stepped back inside his apartment. A French press sat on the counter in the kitchen, his coffee steeping. After pouring a cup, he moved to the sofa, powered up his MacBook Air, and began his daily search for Sarah.

When the *Toronto Sun* newspaper picked up the story of a murder on the CN Tower a few days ago—the death of a Toronto police officer's daughter—images of the shooter were vague and grainy. One video popped up on YouTube, but authorities were trying to suppress any more leaks and imposed a publication ban within twenty-four hours of the incident.

Why a publication ban?

From the grainy photo, Aaron was sure the shooter was Sarah.

He had called Caleb and Amelia, Sarah's parents. Last they heard, Sarah had flown to Toronto to see him after stopping to do something for Vivian.

A little something for Vivian?

That didn't sound good.

Aaron had called Parkman. All Parkman knew was that Sarah wanted to talk to Aaron. Parkman was concerned that Aaron hadn't heard from her yet. Her plane had landed four days before.

Aaron discouraged Parkman from coming to Toronto.

"We can't always drop and run when Sarah goes

underground," Aaron had said. "She has to get used to that. We've all talked about this before."

"I understand, Aaron," Parkman said. "But if Sarah shot a cop's daughter in front of all those witnesses—and don't forget that police officers witnessed the shooting, too—then she's going to need all the help we can offer."

"Come when she turns up, then. Come when she calls. My suggestion is to leave it be for now. I'm here. I'll locate her. Once I do, I'll get back to you."

They had ended the call with the understanding that Aaron would stay in touch daily and apprise Parkman of any developments. Aaron would keep her parents in the loop as well.

Since then, nothing had surfaced. No word from her, no message, no sightings, and no one talking at the police department. Parkman had friends in Toronto from a case he helped with back when a group of fanatics called The Rapturites roamed the streets. The Rapturites killed a lot of cops in a mall food court. Parkman's help, along with Sarah, gave him a lot of credit with the Toronto police, but even he couldn't get anything from them when he called to inquire about the case. All he got were two names. Detectives Niles Mason and Marina Diner. Neither were returning Parkman's calls nor Aaron's.

According to the news website, the cop's daughter, Vanessa Simmons, was being buried today. Her funeral would've already occurred in a small ceremony in a downtown cemetery.

His coffee cup was empty, and each news site scrutinized for any mention of Sarah but finding nothing of value, Aaron got up from the couch to jump in the shower.

The phone rang while he was toweling off.

He dropped the towel and ran for the bedroom phone.

"Hello?" he gasped into the receiver, hoping it was Sarah or Parkman with news.

"Hello, Aaron."

Sarah!

He'd know that voice anywhere.

"Are you okay?" He paused at the sound of exterior noise coming through the phone. "I hear wind. Are you in a car?"

"I'm downtown. John Street. I need you." She cleared her throat. "I came to Toronto to see you. We need to get together. But something has come up that I have to deal with first. I didn't want to involve you, but ..."

"What do you need?" he blurted out, happy she asked him to step up and be there for her.

"Come to Hooters on John Street. No questions right now. I'll tell you everything as soon as this is over. Deal?"

"Fair enough. As long as you tell me you're all right."

"I'm fine." She cleared her throat again. "There's a white Dodge Charger parked out front of Hooters. It's my rental. I left the keys in it. They're under the mat. Get in. Drive to the large shopping mall on Yonge Street. You know, the one where all those cops died in the food court. Use the Shuter Street entrance to access the parking garage. Find somewhere to park on the second level. I'll meet you there within an hour or so."

"Okay, I can do that."

"Come and take the car now. There's no more time to talk. You have ten minutes, maybe more. Move the car as soon as you get here. Don't look for me. It's too dangerous. If the authorities are standing around the car, leave. Just keep walking. I'll be in touch. Otherwise, I'll see you in the mall's parking garage in an hour or so."

"How will you know how to find me in the mall?"

"Vivian."

"Right."

"Gotta go. Move the car. Now."

The line died.

Aaron checked the time on the wall clock over his TV. Relieved to have heard her voice and be in a position to help, Aaron dressed while calling a taxi and bolted from the apartment in under two minutes, his hair still wet, wavy, and unkempt.

He would make it close to ten minutes, but inside fifteen for sure.

Maybe he was wrong about Sarah. A man can make mistakes. Life had been quiet, almost boring without her. Or was this love he felt? The yearning for her, the need—not just need, desire—to do whatever she wanted him to do on a moment's notice. It was like a calling that made him feel good simply by answering. Her voice, the supple resonance, and the melodic quality gave him goosebumps. Everything about her just oozed love.

Maybe it was love that made him walk away from her in California. Maybe he loved her too much. It hurt that bad to see her tormented, her life in peril.

But if this was love, what's next? How far would he go for her, and could he continue to be by her side regardless of what she does for Vivian?

The better question was if she loved him back. Was she in Toronto to meet with him to let *him* go? Or was she just working for Vivian?

All in good time. All in good time.

First, move the car.

Then they would have a coffee, maybe dinner, and see where things went from there.

They'd be back together like before if he had a choice, but no one decided that for Sarah.

Only Sarah decided for Sarah.

And that was what scared him.

Chapter 5

Detective Timothy Simmons entered The Office and scanned the small pub. The woman in braids from the cemetery sat in the back corner, the last table. It looked like she was texting someone on her cell phone or had just ended a call.

To his left, one table was occupied by a young couple. On his right, two women chatted quietly, red wine before them. The rest of the patrons were on the patio, enjoying the nice weather. Someone had turned the air conditioner up high in the early afternoon heat and hadn't adjusted it as the sun moved behind the skyscrapers. He shivered with the temperature contrast from the outside.

He pulled out his cell phone and flipped it to vibrate as he made his way to the back to join Erzabet if that was her real name.

At the table, he gestured for her to stand. Without

looking at him, she rose and thrust her arms out.

He frisked her, looking for concealed weapons or a listening device. She was clean except for the cell phone. No purse, no wallet. Nothing in her pockets except for two twenty-dollar bills. Not even car keys.

Where the hell is she hiding those?

She didn't protest when he grabbed her cell phone.

He paused at a glimmer of something in her eye when he grabbed her phone. He'd seen that look before in the eyes of hardened criminals, gang bangers, and serial killers. A look of hatred, violence. Like she could rip his eyes out with her bare hands and stomp on his throat just because she thought it was what was needed.

He cautioned himself to be extra careful around her, wary of her actions and who she had for backup if backup existed. But the look in this girl's eyes told him she didn't need backup. She could handle whatever came at her with ease.

Quickly, to avoid escalating the tension further, he scanned through her previous calls and text messages, but there was nothing to see. She must have sent something or called someone and then erased it as he walked in. Asking her about it was fruitless, so he handed her phone back.

They sat in the booth at the same time.

He adjusted his jacket, so the side with the gun was open, ready.

"Talk," he said.

"Questions first," she replied.

Her eyes moved. They stopped on his lower face, rose, and met his eyes. They had a power of their own. In the dim light at the back of the restaurant, her eyes had an elliptical feel to them, cunning like cat's eyes. He reminded himself to be cool, to play this right.

"You're a detective. Correct?" she asked.

Tim nodded. He placed his hands on the table.

"What have you *detected* about your daughter's case?"

A waitress approached from behind the bar.

"What can I get ya?" she asked.

Her nametag read Gigi.

"Water for now, Gigi," Tim said. "Give us ten minutes to talk after that. Then we'll order."

They waited in silence until Gigi returned with water. When she started away, Tim leaned into the table.

"Why bring me here to ask about a case I'm not assigned to? You know a lot about me. I'm sure you know they wouldn't let me investigate the murder of my own daughter."

Against his will, not wanting to show weakness, his eyes watered at the thought of Vanessa.

"I think I know who ordered the hit," she said.

"It was a hit?" he asked, incredulity in his voice. "Why? What had Vanessa done?"

Erzabet studied his face. He waited as she scrutinized him like she was attempting to determine the last time he shaved.

"What?" he finally said.

"You're not lying."

His heart raced in his chest like a broken-winged bird. If he checked his blood pressure, he was sure it would be off the charts. Everything about this girl was such a mystery. Was she a friend or foe? Could she help him or not?

She acted calm and relaxed like this was some kind of game to her.

"Of course, I'm not lying," he said. "How could I be?

You haven't asked me anything I can lie about."

"You didn't know what Vanessa was into," she said, more a statement than a question.

He sat back in his seat and pressed his unbroken palm against the table's edge.

"Then tell me. What has my daughter been doing?"

The girl searched his face again, then said, "No."

"And why not? Isn't this why we're here?"

She shook her head slowly, resolutely. "It isn't. I needed to learn how much you know. Now I know."

It was his turn to shake his head. He sputtered when he said, "What?"

"Tell me something."

He waved his hand for her to go ahead. Since they began talking, Erzabet had brought her arms up and rested them on the top of the table, spread out.

"Why would she be afraid of cremation?"

"Who? Vanessa?"

Erzabet nodded.

"I have no idea why she would be afraid of cremation—" he stopped as a cold snake slithered down his spine, forcing a cool sheen of sweat to bead on his forehead. His stomach felt like someone had placed a block of ice in it, and his legs suddenly weakened.

Cremation.

That was how his associates disposed of their victims when they were used up. He didn't know where they did it, but he had heard about it. Fire removes all evidence. Dead body disposal was often credited to chemicals. Others chopped body parts into bite-sized portions and fed them to pigs, but his associates simply cremated the bodies.

He didn't need to know where they did it. In fact, he didn't need to know much about their business activities. For the princely sum of a few thousand dollars per month—which always depended upon the quality of the product determined by them—all he needed to do was offer one girl's name and location per month. A hooker. A drug user. Someone with teeth and a few looks but without local family or connections. The prettier they were, with the least amount of attachments, netted him larger sums of money. He had to make sure the choice was from the dregs of society, though, then he was in the clear. No one really cared when a prostitute went missing. They looked around and some stapled posters on street lights, people read about it in the news, but search parties are only formed for children and politicians' kids. Unless the parents of the hooker formed a search party themselves. People disappeared all the time. He saw it as easy money while he was doing his job of helping society out. Why not? Taking shit off the streets was a form of police work, after all.

Once he had fucked up, though. They withheld three months' worth of payments. A runaway he sent them was traced back to a small town in northern Saskatchewan. Her parents were deceased, and she had no siblings. But that ID was fake. She was the daughter of a Toronto businessman. When she turned up missing, the heat was unbearable. The mayor, a crack smoker himself, all the way down to the average grocery store clerk, wanted this girl found. A lot of fingers were pointed. Accusations flew. The police department took a hit as that girl was never found. A jar with her ashes was delivered to him with a note attached. It said the business would stay the same minus three months' payments as he owed them for his mistake. The next mistake would carry more severe consequences.

Shock settled in over his system as the woman across from him glared intensely into his eyes. He felt the blood leave his face as he blanched. Could Vanessa's murder be a result of another mistake he unwittingly made? If it was, whether he spent the rest of his life in jail or died for his efforts, he would expose the consortium. He would shed light on everyone involved, at least as much as he could discover before they stopped him. His contact was a phone number that was texted to him on the first of each month in conjunction with the drop of the money in cash in an envelope at his residence. The text always asked for a name. Prepared, he would text back the one he had chosen for that month.

Once, he traced the number and discovered it was a prepaid phone that was never used before and never again. The only other time this organization came up in conversation was when one of his colleagues drank too much at the yearly Christmas party. He remembered it like it was yesterday. Mark Hemmings. Four in the morning. Whiskey in hand, staggering drunk, crying, and asking if he would be forgiven. When Tim asked what he was talking about, Mark ranted on about the group that whores women out to the right customer at the right price. Men who want to torture a woman, shit on her, or beat the shit out of her, anything to help deal with their mommy issues, was all for the taking at the right price. Some women were simply tied to a bed and offered for free, like an hors d'oeuvre at a costume party to the waiting customers. Mark had paid a sum to gain entry. Once inside, you *must taste the wares or* never leave the place. He saw what was available and did something unspeakable that he wouldn't voice at that Christmas party, but he was obviously struggling to live with his indiscretion.

He repeated over and over that no girl ever leaves their control. The only way it ends is in cremation. It all ends in death, he had said.

That was the last Tim ever saw of Mark Hemmings. The officer disappeared a week later. There was still a missing persons file with his name on it. The case had gone cold.

An innocuous name popped into his head. The Club. As far as he could remember, Mark had called the place The Club or something like that. Maybe that was the consortium, the group Tim sent women to. If so, he wanted no part in it. The Club was dangerous and catered to the elite, the rich. There was a reason the place wasn't closed down.

Tim tried to breathe, to collect himself. He looped his fingers around the glass of water, brought it to his mouth, and drank, spilling some over his lips. It dripped onto his chest. He steadied himself and set the glass down.

While he thought back to what he knew about the consortium and whether he had made another mistake or not, he considered the girl sitting across from him. Obviously, a professional. If she was with them and had a message for him, he would hear it and kill her where she sat. At least he would save her the trouble of being cremated. If she wasn't with them, then who was she? And why was she here?

"You've lost color," she said. "You're shaking, sweating. It appears you know what cremation means and why Vanessa would fear it."

"No, I mean yes, but I don't see how it's connected to …"

"You're not making sense."

The waitress started toward them. Erzabet waved her off.

"There's no rational reason for Vanessa to fear it," he said.

"Then why did you nearly shit yourself when I said cremation?"

"How did you come by this information? How did you know Vanessa? And how do you know about me and what pub I used to go to? Out at the cemetery, you said, 'I know who ordered the kill.' Tell me then, who was it? Who ordered the murder of my daughter?"

Erzabet's eyes seemed to glaze over. He waited, each second torture. He wanted to rip the answers out of her throat but knew he needed to stay calm and wait.

The girl opened her mouth. Closed it, then opened it and said, "The last thing Vanessa said to me was, 'It all ends in death. I refuse to be cremated.' What do you think that means?"

Tim slammed his fist onto the table loud enough for the two women behind him to eke out a startled yip.

"This isn't a fucking game." He leaned across the table, eyes watering. "Tell me how you're connected. When was the last time you saw Vanessa? Were you the last one to see her alive?"

Ignoring his outburst as if his temper was a child's tantrum, Erzabet leaned closer to his face. "Vanessa said that her death would stop the raping, the degradation, humiliation, and the torture. What could that mean?"

He leaned back in his seat and pulled out his weapon. Once she had seen it, he lowered it below the table.

"I will leave this pub in a few minutes with answers. If I

don't, I will still leave, but you will have new holes in your body to help you think about how you fucked with the wrong guy."

Her expression didn't change. That was so unusual in his line of work. People always shitted themselves at the sight of a gun pointed at them, the weapon holder ready to use it. Her eyes were absent of fear, nor did he see an ounce of nervousness. She acted as if he was pointing a paper origami gun at her, folded nicely and painted a metallic gray.

"What are you mixed up in, Detective Timothy Simmons?"

At that moment, he realized he had miscalculated her. She was another cop, maybe Special Investigations Unit. Could she be investigating the consortium? If so, was it possible that she had interviewed Vanessa and explained what the consortium was and how he received monthly payments for his involvement? Of course, that would lead Vanessa to suicide, but murder … who would murder her? The consortium? But why?

He eased back in his seat, unclear on his next move.

Erzabet slipped sideways to get up from the table.

"Where are you going?" he asked. "We're not done here."

"As long as you're pointing a weapon at me, we're done."

He counted two breaths before he aimed it at the ceiling and eased it back inside his jacket.

"Fine. Sit. We'll talk. We may have a common goal."

The girl shot her fist across his face in a blur, knocking him sideways in his seat. Before he could recover and sit up, she jabbed open-palmed at his broken left hand. He screamed and pulled his hand into his body, the pain incredible.

She grabbed his hair and yanked his head back until he was blinded by the lights in the pub ceiling.

Her lips caressed his ear as she whispered, "Don't ever pull a gun on me again unless you intend to use it. I'm here to bring them all down. That means you, too. Prepare yourself for a shit storm. I'm all out of kid gloves. No more fucking around."

She thrust his head forward so fast his forehead smashed into the table, bouncing once. She was already walking out the door when he righted himself and turned around.

He wiped the spittle from his mouth, got out of his seat as best he could, holding his broken hand, and ran for the door. Two chairs were in his way as he stumbled across the pub.

"Are you okay, Mister?" the waitress asked as he passed her.

Without saying a word, he crashed through the door, gun firmly in hand.

The Charger was gone. But that was impossible. He made it to the door in the time she would've needed to get across the street. No way she could've gotten in the car, turned it on—he hadn't heard it start—and driven away. At this hour, John Street was busy. Car after car drove by. How did she pull that off?

"Mister, would you like me to call anyone for you?"

Tim let the door close behind him. He needed painkillers. That fucking girl probably broke his hand again. Lightheadedness swept over him. He staggered as he walked down the sidewalk toward the underground parking garage.

He would run her plate number when he got to the office.

He would text questions when the consortium contacted him for a name and a location. He would come to the bottom of this and hurt that girl when he saw her again.

He stumbled down the access ramp into the parking garage and turned toward his car. The driver's side window was busted in. Glass littered the concrete by his car door, sparkling like little diamonds. He scanned the empty garage. Not even the sound of someone fleeing the area could be heard.

A common thug? Or the girl?

He trudged to his car, the pain in his hand intensifying, throbbing.

Glass covered the driver's seat. He ambled around to the passenger side, unlocked and opened the door, plopping down into the seat. He took a deep, calming breath.

When he opened the glove box, he saw nothing had been disturbed. Whoever broke in must've just wanted to cause damage. Even the CD Player was still there. Nothing else seemed to have been touched.

Like a strobe light going off in his head, he thought of his police gun.

He opened the center console.

It was empty.

The gun was gone.

Who knew it was there? In his unmarked cruiser, he wore the gun. In his personal vehicle, he stored it in the console. Did Erzabet see him place it in there at the cemetery?

No way. She didn't look at him once. She had stoically stared straight ahead the entire time. She didn't look at him until they were seated across from each other in the pub.

Then who did this? And why?

He struggled with it for a full minute but came back to the girl. It had to be her.

It was time to call it in.

He pulled out his phone, called Marina, and told her to bring Niles. Meet him on John Street.

"Bring a lot of Advil," he added before hanging up.

Chapter 6

JAMIE STRATTON CALLED IN his position as he performed a safe walk with Mrs. Jennings. Mrs. Jennings, at least eighty years of age and fragile, shopped at Eaton's Centre every week, filling her basket on wheels and asking security for a safe walk to her car. Eaton's Centre security offered safe walks to anybody who requested one. Ever since the shooting in the food court in 2012, the requests for safe walks had skyrocketed. Sometimes Jamie spent half a shift walking people to their cars.

Today was different, though. Not five minutes ago, Jamie's patrol supervisor had radioed all security guards walking the garage levels to watch for a white Dodge Charger. The police scanner in the main office had announced that all units were to be on the lookout for that vehicle. Jamie had written the plate number down, committed it to memory, and then met Mrs. Jennings at the elevators.

She babbled on about the same things every week. How many kids and grandkids she had, and how they never visited her. With disdain, she said one of them should at least take her shopping to help carry the bags. Once, she said she wished Jamie were her son. A good boy like him, always walking her to her car. His mother should be proud. Mrs. Jennings had no idea that Jamie's mother was dead and his father was an alcoholic. A drunk driver killed his mother, and his father became a drunk. Who would've figured?

But today, he tuned out Mrs. Jennings's babbling. He wanted to be the one to find the Charger if it was in the parking garage. He had recently put in for a raise with Eaton's Centre Security as he waited to hear back from the Durham Regional Police Force on his application. He'd graduated from Grade 12 and was about to start university but thought he'd see if the force was willing to take him now. He figured there was nothing wrong with being overeager.

Mrs. Jennings had parked on the third level. Once she was settled in her car, her bags neatly packed in the trunk, he said his goodbyes, accepted her two-dollar tip—had to, even though it wasn't allowed because she wouldn't entertain protest—and watched as she backed up three times in order to exit the parking space. She was headed down the spiral exit toward Yonge Street a moment later.

Instead of reentering the mall, Jamie decided to walk to the main floor through the garage. Maybe he would get lucky and find the Charger.

On the second floor, he stopped and counted over a dozen white car roofs. He wasn't up on car makes and models yet. That was what notebooks were for.

He opened his and reread the plate number.

Then he started toward the first white roof.

A Challenger. The next one was a four-door BMW. It wasn't until the seventh vehicle that he stopped and stared at it from a distance.

Someone was sitting in the driver's seat. He appeared to be looking at something in his lap. Could be texting on a phone or playing a game while waiting for his wife or girlfriend.

Jamie approached with caution. He stayed two rows over, remaining behind SUVs and larger vehicles. Before walking out into the open and exposing his position, he dropped behind the bumper of a car and lay flat. Then he rolled behind another car and peered between the two at the plate number of the suspect vehicle.

It was like winning the lottery. He couldn't believe his luck. The plate was an exact match. From where he lay, he could read the word Charger on the right side of the trunk.

He had done it. He had solved a crime. Maybe he could put it on his résumé. Durham Regional Police would love to have diligent, intrepid, brave men on their team. He fist-pumped the air and almost punched the exhaust pipe of the car he hid behind.

His radio crackled, and he jumped, smacking his head on the car's bumper in front of him.

He rolled away until he was behind a van and got to his feet.

He radioed in his position and reported finding the white Dodge Charger the police were seeking. The patrol supervisor told him to hold his position while he informed the authorities. No congratulations, no offer of a pat on the back.

Jealousy. That's all that was.

Jamie was going to go places. One day he would make detective while his patrol supervisor would still be a patrol supervisor. Then he would see who gets the pat on the back.

Then he would see.

Chapter 7

TIM WINCED AS THE paramedic examining him prodded his injured hand on the back bumper of an ambulance while Niles and Marina watched.

"You always carry your piece in your personal car?" Niles asked.

He had one of those thick *Magnum P.I.* mustaches from the seventies or eighties. Behind Niles's back, the guys at the station called it a seventies porn 'stache. Tim couldn't help but look at it when Niles talked. It was like a small rodent had died and now lay under Niles's nose.

"Just run the plate number," Tim said. "If we get a hit, we can find the girl and get my gun back."

"I called it in when we got here." Marina cleared her throat and wiped something off her lips. "Certain people upstairs will be pissed you had your piece stolen. That kinda shit goes on your record."

Tim winced as the paramedic pushed at another sensitive spot.

"You almost done?" he asked.

"You're fine," the medic said. "Nothing new broken. The pain'll subside soon. You have something for the pain?"

"Yeah," Tim said as he pushed off the back of the ambulance and walked away.

Officers were taking statements from the waitress and the two women who watched the whole thing. People stood outside businesses across the street; others watched from windows. It was a regular peep show happening on John Street.

John Street.

The irony of the name never hit him before. Imagine a hooker walking John Street.

He laughed to himself.

"Something funny?" Marina asked from behind him. "After burying your daughter this morning, you're down here having a covert meeting, and then—"

He stopped and spun around to look at her as a phone rang. She turned away from him, her cell up to her ear. She appeared to be listening. She nodded, then dropped her phone in a pocket.

"Plates came back. A rental. Enterprise."

"I knew it," Tim said.

Marina frowned and put a hand on her hip. "How did you know?"

"Instinct. Can you get the name off the rental agreement?"

Marina nodded. "Already got it. But it can't be right."

Now it was Tim's turn to frown. "Why not?"

"It doesn't add up. Someone's using a fake name."

Tim stepped toward her, eager to hear the name. "Tell me. Who rented the car?"

"You might remember her. Saved a lot of people in this city a few years in a row."

"Huh?"

"That American psychic girl, Sarah Roberts. Any chance you screwed the number up?"

Tim mumbled, "No chance," as he stumbled away.

"It fits with the shooting," Marina said to her partner Niles. "At least that's what we're working with."

Sarah Roberts?

Not Erzabet. Of course. That's why he recognized her. The braids threw him off. She even used a name that he would match with the braids. She knew his past. His name. She knew about the consortium. She spoke with Vanessa. All because she was psychic or something.

His stomach rolled as his legs weakened for the umpteenth time today. He leaned against a car, panting, his heart smacking against his rib cage.

"You okay?" Marina asked.

"Yeah. The hand's throbbing. Just give me a sec."

If Sarah was here and she knew everything, then he was done. She brought down The Rapturites. She attacked a street gang even the cops were afraid of. The MS-13 or something. Cops retired because of Sarah. He remembered her having friends. Tough guys. Friends on the force and the FBI.

But what was she doing in Toronto? Didn't her boyfriend live here? He couldn't remember everything as he hadn't worked on those cases, but he knew a few cops who worked closely with Sarah. She was an enigmatic vigilante who lived by her own rules. Of course, she would know what to say to him. She would know where he had stashed his gun. Sarah would know everything, and he figured his life was about to change for the worse.

Marina's phone rang. She grabbed it without taking her eyes off Tim.

"Speak." She nodded and smiled. "They sure?" She nodded again. "How did they know about it?" Her eyes moved to Tim. "Scanner. Makes sense. We're on our way. Make sure they stay where they are. Don't let that car leave their sight. I'll be there in minutes."

She jammed her phone in her pocket and turned in a run.

"Who was that?" Tim asked. "Where are you going?"

"They found the Charger."

"Gathered that. Where?"

"Parking garage. Second level. Eaton's Centre." She looked back. "You coming?"

Suddenly his legs had strength again.

"Wait. What did you mean before when you said to Niles that it fit with the shooting?"

"Just that it was Sarah Roberts who shot Vanessa. We have three cell phone recordings that place Sarah at the scene, firing three times into your daughter."

Tim didn't know how much he could take in one day. And how could Marina say what she just said so casually, as if discussing a dead dog on the highway?

"What …" Tim muttered.

"We have her fingerprints on the murder weapon, too. That's why there's a publication ban, and we seized all the recordings at the tower. At least we thought we got them all."

"But why?" Tim asked, stunned, his head beginning to

hurt, throbbing at the temples.

"Sarah's done a lot of good for the people of Toronto. Someone high up wants to hear her side of the story before it all comes out. She's earned some respect around here. I was given this case to make sure she gets that respect."

"Then why tell me now? Why are you bringing me in on this?"

"She involved you, not me. This little meeting took place because she has an agenda, a purpose. Find Sarah, learn what she's up to, and we'll discover why she went after Vanessa. Are you coming or not?"

"Nothing would stop me," he gasped as he breathed in deeply.

He would interview Sarah himself. Assaulting a police officer. Breaking and entering. Stealing his weapon. The last one to see Vanessa alive before she was murdered.

Sarah wasn't psychic. She was full of shit. It was risky meeting him like that. What if he had known what Marina knew?

What could she have gained by talking to him?

He should have shot her. When officers arrived, they would've understood. Sarah Roberts was a murderer, after all.

An eye for an eye. Sarah Roberts had to die.

But before all that, Sarah had a lot of explaining to do, and he was just the one to accept her apology and atonement for what she had done.

Chapter 8

SARAH WALKED UP UNIVERSITY Avenue, then turned down Queen Street and unbraided her hair as she hit Bay Street. Detective Timothy Simmons's gun fit snuggly at the back of her waistband. Vivian hadn't been forthcoming as to why it was necessary to harass the dead girl's father or steal his weapon. When Sarah asked her sister if Tim was responsible in any way for Vanessa's attempted suicide, Vivian replied that Tim had done terrible things that would catch up with him soon enough but that he wasn't holding the smoking gun. Tim's daughter had gotten herself into trouble all on her own. Tim knew the people responsible, but that was the only connection.

One thing Sarah could rely on was the absolute truth from Vivian. But that truth came when Vivian was prepared to offer it.

Sarah was still angry with what Vivian made her do.

Shooting Vanessa with so many witnesses couldn't end well. Sarah could've died jumping from the CN Tower. So many things could've gone wrong. A limit on how much Sarah was willing to trust Vivian appeared on the horizon. It seemed Vivian would do whatever she wanted whenever she wanted, and consequences be damned.

Usually, that was fine with Sarah. That was their foundation, who they were. But unjustified murder? Even in Sarah's angriest moments, Vivian intruded to remind her that Vanessa was dead anyway and murder had been the only way. Suicide kept buried the things Vivian needed to be exposed. Murder opened the proverbial can of worms.

So Sarah kept listening, doing, and performing. Meet Tim at the funeral. Braid hair. Claim to be Erzabet. Question him. Rile him up. Escape his presence, but call Aaron and have the car moved. Steal Tim's gun. Meet Aaron later. The next step happens tomorrow. Blah, blah, blah.

Sarah had done it all and was now one block from the Eaton's Centre parking garage. Vivian had not unveiled the next step or who she would be chasing tomorrow.

Sarah turned south on Yonge toward the Shuter Street entrance to the parking garage when two police cars raced by, sirens off, lights rotating.

She slowed her step.

Three black and whites were coming from the other way with an unmarked cruiser behind them.

Sarah picked up her step again. They couldn't have run the plates, called the rental agency, got the name, and then found where Aaron had parked the car in all of a half hour, could they?

Unless Tim called it in early, and they caught a lucky

break.

Aaron was with the car. He would be waiting for her.

Shit!

She jogged the rest of the way, entered the access door to the parking garage, and took the stairs to the second level two at a time. Once there, the metal door opened without a sound. An inch was all she needed to watch what was taking place. The police cars had surrounded the white Charger. Officers with guns out shouted at the driver of the car to get out with his hands up.

Her fury with Vivian rose for dragging Aaron into this and allowing him to get involved when Sarah had come here to make peace. This was the last thing she needed. Aaron had fled this life and, with one phone call, was being arrested for her.

The car's door moved slowly until it was fully open. A moment later, Aaron's hands rose above the roof of the car as he emerged.

Three officers jumped in, two holding him down while the other cuffed him from behind. One of the officers forced his knee into the back of Aaron's neck. Aaron yowled in pain.

Sarah opened the stairwell door, ready to run at them, but Vivian screamed in her head to stand down. The scream was so sudden and overwhelming that Sarah staggered to her feet. Stunned, she grabbed at the door to avoid dropping to her knees. With one deep breath, she eased back into the stairwell, but not before Aaron's eyes found her.

They stared at each other for a moment before Sarah mouthed the words, *I'm sorry.*

He made a half smile, then blinked his eyes in an I-got-this gesture. Her heart swooned at that moment.

What did they have on him, anyway? Sitting in a car in the parking garage? That wasn't illegal. Sure, it was the car she'd used, but she was the one they were after. He would have an alibi for any questions they threw at him. He had friends, a dojo to run, and students who would corroborate his attendance in class. They had nothing on him. This arrest was a formality. Aaron would be home for dinner.

Maybe that was Vivian's plan since the beginning.

But Sarah didn't have to like it. The people she was close to weren't pawns. Sarah was always willing to do what was necessary, but lately, without using the old method of automatic writing, Vivian could tell Sarah what she wanted whenever she felt like it, which was taking some time to get used to.

They picked Aaron up and placed him in the back of the unmarked cruiser. A tall woman closed the car door and leaned in the passenger window. When she stood back up and walked around to get in the driver's seat, the passenger leaned out the open window.

Timothy Simmons.

He was connected to all of this. When would Vivian let her in on it?

Soon ...

The word echoed throughout her head.

Sarah eased the door closed and headed down the stairs to the sidewalk. Outside, she mingled with a crowd of people and watched as the cruisers, one by one, exited the parking garage.

The unmarked car with Aaron in the back seat emerged from the garage and hung a left. As it passed, she studied the female driver. When she moved her eyes to look at Simmons, he stared back at her.

The car's tires screeched to a stop as the cruiser braked instantly. He'd seen her and recognized her without the braids.

Sarah ducked low, bobbed, and weaved through the crowd until she was in the stairwell again. She ran up, jumping two stairs at a time as she had done ten minutes ago. On the second level, she exited the stairs and headed for the edge to look down on Yonge Street. The passenger door was closing. Tim must've lost sight of her and got back in the car. It started away, Aaron in the back seat.

After watching until she couldn't see it anymore, she entered the mall and exited at the south end. A few blocks up, she found a small bar.

Vivian wanted her to take a Greyhound somewhere just north of a city called Barrie. It was something to do with a summer cottage she was supposed to stake out tomorrow afternoon for some reason.

But tonight, she would stay lost in the stream of thousands of people downtown Toronto. Tonight, she would drink to squash the memory of shooting Vanessa, a young girl with so much life ahead of her. She would drink because she had no idea how many days of freedom she had left.

She felt very unlucky, as if nothing was working out as it should. How could Vivian get a murder charge off her back? What did the police know? They had to have pictures, videos, and eyewitnesses to the shooting. Yet the media weren't publishing much because of a gag order.

She had thought about calling Parkman in, but not now. How Vivian handled the people close to her convinced Sarah to keep Parkman out of this one.

The bar was quiet as the sun hadn't dropped yet. After a few drinks, she would take a taxi to Mississauga. She knew a few hotels that took cash, no ID. After some rest, she would take the bus north of Barrie and stake out the cottage. For what? She still had no idea. But she'd do it because that's who she was. Vivian's pawn.

As she ordered her drink, a thought struck her. Maybe Vivian was withholding something because the information was too horrible. After all that Sarah had seen and been through, what could be so bad that Vivian felt the need to shield her from it?

Just trust me ...

The echo of those words made her call the bartender back.

"Cancel that wine I ordered. I need whiskey. Make it a double and keep the bottle close. I need to drown out the voices in my head."

"Coming right up, lady."

Chapter 9

With every cop in Toronto looking for Sarah, taking public transportation was risky. The Greyhound ticket to Barrie was already bought in her name, but instead of using it, she took a cab to the Toronto International Airport and hired a black limo—not the stretch kind—to drive her to Casino Rama in Orillia. Just short of her destination, she told the driver to pull over and let her out. She paid the full amount and started walking.

The cloudless sky offered a rich shade of blue, the sun high and blazing its heat down upon the concrete she walked, sweat oozing from her every pore. Eyes half-lidded, she lumbered along the road, hoping today wouldn't require much physical work.

Vivian had explained where to go in a version of psychic magnetism. The image of the cottage Sarah was supposed to stake out was planted in her mind like a photo. The location was offered in a way that Sarah knew where to go by moving forward—which was a strange feeling. If she headed away from the cottage, an internal compass, a yearning to turn back, coursed through her. Until she reached her destination, this internal guide led her to the cottage just south of Orillia without explaining why.

"What's this for, Vivian?" she asked out loud.

The concession road she walked along was dirty, the pavement broken and disheveled in places. A sign on her right said *Frost Heaves*, which probably explained the decrepit look of the back road.

The heat didn't help with her throbbing head. Even after three painkillers, her whiskey headache had only dimmed slightly, leaving a subtle throbbing between the temples.

Served her right for trying to block Vivian's voice. It seemed she couldn't detect Vivian's presence when she was quite sloshed. The more she drank, the further the voice moved into the far recesses of her consciousness and the more Sarah got herself back. Ultimately, all that was achieved was a drunk Sarah without Vivian's protection. That was scary and made her feel vulnerable in its own way, but it was also liberating.

The year before, she had learned whiskey meant something like *water for life* in Gaelic. She could use some water now as her tongue was an arid piece of meat flopping around in her mouth.

It wasn't the brightest idea to get drunk in Toronto, either. Not while every authority on every block hunted her.

They probably still had Aaron locked up, drilling a thousand questions at him. And they wouldn't believe him when they learned he was her boyfriend but had only heard from her recently under mysterious circumstances. How could Sarah be in Toronto and her own boyfriend didn't know about it? *Where is she?* they'd ask. *Why is she here?* Aaron was tough, but they would push him hard.

When this was over, she would find a way to make it up to him if he'd let her.

Shrubs, bushes, and trees surrounded the concession road. Not a single leaf moved in the still air. The sound of the highway grew dimmer as she walked away from it.

After five minutes, a green car came toward her. The female driver checked her out, staring longer than normal. Sarah paid the driver no extra attention. There was a cottage Vivian was leading her to. Focus on that. Watch the place. Then leave and get water. And more sleep.

After fifteen minutes, a tall fence came up on the right. A cool slither moved down her back, a chill in the heat for a brief moment. She slowed her step.

Is this the place?

Sarah didn't need an answer. She knew what she was looking at. That all-knowing feeling, strange as it was, returned.

She had found the cottage. It was surrounded by a fence topped with barbed wire.

"How do I get in?" she asked out loud.

The urge to move forward swept over her. Putting one foot in front of the other, Sarah followed the fence until she reached a corner where the road turned to the right.

Detective Simmons's gun had slipped slightly in the sweat at the back of her pants. She pulled it out, checked that the safety was off, and held it aimed at the sky as she eased around the corner. A large iron gate sat open. Atop this gate, barbed wire was twirled in circles like the fences at concentration camps.

How can I watch the cottage from outside the gate?

Enter quietly in half a minute, came the reply, echoing in that resonant cadence of Vivian's voice. Even though Vivian had occupied her body, made her pass out and write notes, saved her life countless times, and now talked directly to her in this fashion, it still took some getting used to. Sarah had the urge to shake her head as if a mosquito buzzed close by when Vivian whispered to her. Only recently had she been able to resist that urge, knowing how it would look to others.

The clock ticked. The gate remained open.

Maybe the woman who drove by minutes before had come from here, leaving the gate ajar.

Then why wait, Vivian?

At least twenty seconds had passed. Sarah decided to move forward. She stepped out from behind the corner and heard footsteps approaching almost immediately.

She pivoted on her heels and jumped back behind the security of the wall where she had been hiding moments before.

A man emerged from the opening in the gate. He walked with purpose, his face glued to the phone in his hand. White cords fed from the phone to his ears. As she watched him, the man touched something in his pocket, and the large iron gate began to close.

She waited, judging how far away he would get before the gate closed completely. The gate was slow, but if she ran through now, all he had to do was turn around to see her out in the open.

But the gate was almost closed now.

Go! Sarah winced and tightened a fist at the loud shout in her head. As she opened her eyes, she jumped from hiding, ran the short distance to the opening in the gate, and hopped out of sight of the road. A moment later, the gate closed, clunking into place with finality.

Like the sound of a busy beehive, a buzzing hum started the second the gate closed.

Electricity. The fence was wired. *What the hell for? What are they afraid might get in?*

Sarah turned around slowly on the gravel driveway and surveyed the cottage's façade.

Or better yet, what are they afraid will get out?

On the outside, the building appeared to be like any other in these parts. Big for a cottage, though. She headed to the side of the four-level side split fully detached house. Something told her—whether it was Vivian or her intuition—that the house lacked hostiles. Knowing she could relax, she eased the gun back into her belt line and began to examine the building from the outside.

Ten minutes later, other than uncut grass, dirty windows, and a ratty interior—whoever lived here didn't keep a clean home—Sarah took one of the Adirondack chairs from the back porch and carried it up to the small thatch of trees on the side corner of the lot for shade. She cursed herself for not having brought water. There was nothing she could do about it now. When this stake-out task was done, she would drink a keg of water, pouring half of it over her face and body. Then she would pop more painkillers and get some rest.

And lay off the whiskey, she thought.

She found a spot in the trees that gave her a clear view of the front gate. Shrouded as she was in deep shade, anyone coming in the gate wouldn't readily see her, nor would they know to look her way.

Her head back, feet out, she crossed her hands on her stomach and closed her eyes. A catnap would help. The residents could have gone to work and wouldn't return until evening.

A voice startled her. She jerked awake and sat up.

It sounded like someone had pleaded for help. The gate was still closed, the electricity humming softly. The air was still. Only the distant sound of the highway reached her. She waited, breathing slowly in order to listen. Whatever the noise was, it didn't come again.

Must've been in my head.

She leaned back in the chair and kept her eyes open as long as she could. Eventually, they closed, and Sarah fell asleep.

When the call for help came from the house again, she was too far under to hear it.

Chapter 10

BELINDA MCCARTHY SANG ALONG with the music of Toronto band Moxy Früvous as they boasted through her car stereo speakers about being the King of Spain as she drove along Highway 11.

Thirty more kilometers until her turn, the music loud, window open, the wind rushing past her face, hair blowing over her shoulder in the wind. Nothing better than a summer drive toward Rama.

Casino Rama, on the other side of Orillia, Ontario, had filled this part of Highway 11 with traffic since it opened in the nineties. People from southern Ontario flooded the road, racing north, hoping to pop the big one and living on an easy street afterward.

But Belinda knew different. There was no easy street. There was only life and what you made of it. Instead of hoping a fortuitous win would come your way or lightning would strike, why not set out and take from life what you want? Only then could you be truly happy.

She sang louder; the cigarette clutched between her yellowed fingers forgotten, the ashes about to meet her flesh. A quick flick of her wrist and the butt was out the window, flying under the wheels of an eighteen-wheeler going by.

The highway bent on a long arc as it passed a farm. Up ahead on the right, a lone female stood, a bag at her feet, thumb up and out.

Belinda hit her blinker, intent on adding the hitchhiker to her party. The passenger seat was occupied by a bag containing three bottles of wine. They jostled against each other as she lifted the bag over the front seat and set it in the baby seat in the back. She wouldn't need the baby seat today. She lowered the volume and pulled onto the shoulder.

The hitchhiker was already grabbing her bag as Belinda eased closer. The wind from a rig going by shook the car.

She waved through the windshield as the hitchhiker walked toward her vehicle. Drawing close, the woman slowed, glancing through the windows to see if Belinda was alone. Closer still, Belinda saw the girl's eyes rimmed in red, a purple bruise on the edge of her mouth.

What happened to her?

The girl walked past the car door and bent to look in the back. The baby seat must've signed the deal because the hitchhiker opened the passenger door and dropped in the seat, her bag on her lap. Before closing the door and fully committing to the ride, she met Belinda's eyes.

"I'm safe, darlin'," Belinda said. "Shut the door, and I'll take ya where ya need to go."

The door closed, but the girl kept her hand on the knob as

if she would bolt at any moment.

Belinda pulled off the gravel shoulder and eased back into traffic, getting the car up to the posted limit.

"Where ya headed?" she asked.

"North."

The girl's voice sounded fragile, broken. Someone had done a number on this girl. She was running; that much was for sure. How much money did she have? How long could she run before whoever was looking for her caught up?

"You okay, darlin'?" Belinda said as she snuck a glance sideways.

Her foot eased off the pedal to reduce her speed. She wanted more time to talk to the girl, loosen her up, and hear her story.

She grabbed her cigarette pack, popped one in her mouth, and fished the lighter from her center console.

"You mind?" Belinda asked.

The girl shook her head back and forth in a quick, short burst.

"You want one, be my guest."

That quick short burst again.

Belinda rolled her window up and eased the volume of Moxy off a little more.

"What's your name?" she asked.

"Isabel." It came out in a throaty voice like she had just come from a heavy metal concert where she had screamed along with the music for far too long.

"Isabel. I like that." Belinda pulled on the smoke, inhaled, waited a moment, then blew it out. She flicked the ashes off in the ashtray. "Nice name."

After another moment of silence, Belinda said, "You like

music?"

The girl nodded. She was calming and relaxing. Like she was reading Belinda's vibe and beginning to let go. That was a good thing. That was what Belinda wanted.

"You ever heard of a band called Moxy Früvous?"

"No," Isabel said.

That was an improvement. Better than those violent headshakes.

"Here. Listen."

Belinda turned them back up. The band was going through their song called "My Baby Loves A Bunch Of Authors." She hummed along.

"They're good, eh?" Belinda asked.

The girl attempted to smile, a subtle nod this time. She leaned back in her seat, her eyes heavy, and rested her head against the window.

In a distant part of Belinda's mind, she knew this girl's story without having to ask. On the run. Didn't sleep well last night. Going on energy reserves because she hadn't eaten well in days. Red-rimmed eyes due to lack of sleep and nourishment. Constantly afraid, fearful of all the people she meets. Which was a good thing, a survival thing.

And the girl was pretty, too. Very pretty.

Someone had tried to control this girl, to own her. She had too much beauty to be unprotected in this dog-eat-dog world. Belinda knew all about that. Been there, done that. She didn't buy the farm. She owned it.

"Hey, got a question for ya," Belinda said.

The girl sprang up into a straight-backed sitting position, clasping her bag tight enough to whiten her knuckles.

"I don't know your story, and you don't have to tell it to

me." Belinda waited while a pickup truck drove by with one of those modified mufflers that were so loud, the end of it big enough to fit a softball in with room to spare. "But I can see you're in need of some good rest and some food. Come by my place. Stay a few days. Get cleaned up. Stay longer if you like, or leave. It's up to you." The girl remained quiet. "Oh, don't worry about the kid that sits in that baby seat. My ex-husband has our daughter for a two-week vacay. I'm all alone. Nothing to worry about at my place unless chickens spook ya."

They rounded another bend in the road. Belinda's turn-off was coming up on the right within five kilometers.

"You got an answer?" Belinda asked, then inhaled another long draw off her smoke. She rolled the window down and blew the smoke out.

"I … can't," the girl said. "Sorry."

"Oh, no problem. Just trying to help."

"Thanks, though."

Belinda snuck another glance. A tear cleared a path through the road dust and dirt that had gathered on the girl's cheeks.

She stared forward to avoid causing the hitchhiker any more embarrassment than needed, keeping her eyes on the road.

Another hitchhiker came into view, his back to the cars, his thumb out.

"Let's pick this guy up." She was already slowing down. "Let's see where he's going. Who knows? He might be very good-looking."

Fear masked the young girl's pretty face as she leaned into the window, moving her head back and forth.

"It's okay," Belinda cooed. "There's two of us and only one of him." She was on the shoulder now, slowing to a stop behind the man in tight blue jeans. He hadn't turned around yet. "If you're not taking me up on my offer of a free place to stay, at least let me pick up another hitchhiker in my car. After all, it is my car. C'mon, it'll be fun."

The man slowed his step and stopped. He turned around as he yanked earphones out of his ears. His smile parted an unshaven face and displayed yellowed teeth. He brought something to his mouth, held it there, then blew smoke out before dropping it and grinding the toe of a boot on it.

Belinda stole a look at the girl's face, eyes, and mouth to see how she was responding to the male in their windshield.

It didn't look like she would bolt from the car. Maybe the girl was willing to let things slide, and staying in the car meant she got farther away from whatever she was running from.

The man smiled and strode to the back door. He got in the back seat, closed the door, and relaxed back in the seat as if it was his car.

"Afternoon, ladies," he said. "Where're you headed?"

"Better question," Belinda said, "is where are you headed? You were the one thumbing for a ride."

She leaned her head down conspiratorially, winked, and smiled at the young girl across from her.

"I'm headed into Orillia," he said. "Going to see the folks."

"We can take you to any exit you want, but we're heading north. Sorry, it looks like this ride will be a short one for you."

Belinda pulled out onto the highway and got to the speed

of traffic quickly.

On the exit before Orillia, she slowed and turned onto a concession road. The girl beside her instantly grew agitated. Belinda watched from the corner of her eye as the girl fidgeted and clutched her bag close to her chest. She counted down the seconds until the girl spoke. With each passing second, as the highway grew dim in her rearview mirror, Belinda felt surprise mixed with joy. She was happy with their find today. The girl would make a good participant in their games. And she was astounded there had been no protest yet.

Joel eased across the back seat. Belinda studied his form in the mirror, watching her man prepare for the protests that always came when stealing a life.

A lot of people went fishing up in these parts, and Belinda and Joel weren't strangers to fishing themselves. They just went after bigger fish, ones that provided more than the meat surrounding their ribs.

The girl turned to address Belinda. "Where? Where are we going now?"

"Home, little girl. I'm taking you to your new home."

Joel slipped the garrote around the hitchhiker's neck from behind her and pulled her back into the seat. He leaned forward until his lips were beside the girl's ears as she clawed at her throat.

Over her grunts and protests, Joel said, "Fight, little bitch, fight." He looked at Belinda. "I love the ones with a little fight in them. Makes me *real* hard. You like that, too, Belinda?"

"Oh yeah, baby. This bitch looks like she'll go a few rounds."

The hitchhiker's face had turned red, eyes bulging. Belinda slowed and waited for their large iron gate to ease open. Then she turned onto their property as the girl's fight dwindled, her lips a hue of purple now.

Joel eased off the garrote to allow some airflow as the gates behind the car closed.

"Get her out of the car," Joel ordered. "I need a snack before dinner, and this girl will do just fine. But Belinda, don't clean her up. I like 'em dirty. Just strip her and place her in the cellar with the others. Chain her up beside doll face."

Once he was out of the car, he tore the passenger door open and grabbed the hitchhiker's hair, yanking her out and onto the gravel driveway. Then he hollered in the quiet summer morning as the female hitchhiker curled into a ball, sobbing, her strength to fight back diminished by the garrote's brutality.

"Damn," Joel yelled. "I love 'em young, and I love when they cry. Look out, Paul Bernardo. I'm gonna make a name for myself in this province. How about them apples, eh?"

Chapter 11

Someone screamed. Dreams of fistfights and guns did nothing to wake her. Even someone shouting was lost in the fantasy of the dream. Then out of the ether, Vivian's face shot forward. She opened her mouth until it reached impossible proportions. The shout that emanated from Vivian's open gape snapped Sarah awake so fast she slipped out of the Adirondack chair and landed on her ass. She winced and rolled to the side as Detective Simmons's gun poked the base of her spine.

When she rolled to the side, she saw a green car in the driveway. A cool sweat covered her body like it was attempting to force the toxins from last night's whiskey out of her pores. She shuddered in the shade of the pine trees and turned until she could see the car without being seen too easily herself.

It was the green car that had passed her on the way to the

house. The lone female driver got out and slammed her door. She had been in the driveway for at least a full minute before Sarah woke because the iron gate was already closed. The buzzing of the electrified fence radiated through the still summer morning.

Who yelled, then?

The woman walked around to the other side of the car and bent out of sight. She reappeared with something in her hand, but Sarah couldn't see what.

Walking forward, pulling something, the driver's full body came into view. Horrified at what the woman pulled behind her, Sarah almost yanked the weapon and fired a shot off but knew she would probably miss or hit the girl being dragged from this distance.

The pleas and the begging were hard to hear. The woman on the gravel tried to gain her feet, but the driver was relentless in her grip and determination to drag her victim into the house.

A door slammed somewhere inside the house.

Someone else was here.

Was the male who left through the gate with the cell phone and earplugs back?

"Baby?" a man shouted from somewhere near the back of the house. "Where's the chair?"

The chair?

Sarah looked behind her.

Could he be referring to this chair?

If so, how could he know it was missing so fast?

She rolled away from the chair and stood up behind a tree.

The man stepped out onto the back deck and looked

around.

He grunted something and ran back into the house. The voices that came from the inside the house were garbled and disjointed. Sarah couldn't make anything out.

Fully awake now, gun in hand, Sarah waited until they came looking for the chair.

Hey, thanks for waking me, sis.

The back door banged open. The man came into view carrying a long-barreled rifle with a scope. He rested it in the crook of his shoulder, brought the scope to his eye, and began a sweep of the large backyard, following the fence line. Sarah waited until he aimed it close to the copse of trees she had chosen to rest in, then ducked down and remained out of sight.

She kept her back to a tree, breathing slowly. No sounds came from the house. No screams, no shouting, no footsteps, nothing. Not knowing what was happening behind her, she checked the weapon's safety and prepared for what was coming.

Adrenaline pumped through her stomach, her headache a distant tremor. The short rest in the chair had cleared her head some and made her feel better. But her thirst had intensified like she had been gnawing on sand.

A twig snapped close by.

Shit!

The man had seen the chair. He knew someone was out here. There weren't a lot of places to hide. Maybe three trees wide enough to cover someone from the house. His gun would be ready. That left her options very limited.

Vivian? Ideas?

Nothing came to her. No internal voice of solace or

wisdom.

Thanks for the help ...

After two quick breaths, Sarah dropped to the pine needle-covered ground, lay out flat, and rolled away from the tree, arms extended, Simmons's gun thrust outward and pointing in the direction she thought the man would be.

Like a whip cracking the air, the rifle fired from five feet away. The bullets shot up dirt less than one foot from Sarah's face. By the time he readied the rifle to fire again, she had squeezed the trigger of her weapon, aiming low. A leg wound would suffice. The thought of killing again so soon after Vanessa's murder, even in self-defense, made her consider her freedom—or soon lack thereof—as the authorities were already hunting her for one murder.

The bullet almost missed him, entering his inner thigh. But it was enough to make him stumble back. Sarah prepared to fire again but quickly realized she didn't have to. He staggered on his feet, the rifle no longer a threat as he let it dangle by its strap.

It was so quiet this far in the country that Sarah could hear a door slam in the house. She wanted to look. Maybe the woman had her own rifle, now aimed in her general direction.

Blood gushed from the leg wound. Sarah looked at the house when the man dropped the rifle in the dirt. The woman was on the back porch, her hands covering her mouth.

The man dropped to his knees, then tilted to the side until he fell over. The blood had a life of its own as it shot out in pumping actions, matching his pulse.

I hit an artery. Shit!

She got up and raced to his side. His eyes pleaded, wide

and watery. He breathed in ragged gasps as his life source ebbed through his jeans. She glanced at the house again. The woman had disappeared back inside. Probably to get another rifle.

The man grunted, trying to say something.

"Shhh, shhh," Sarah whispered. "Save your strength."

When he walked through the gate earlier, she hadn't paid enough attention to his unshaven face and ragged clothes. He smelled bad, like rancid meat in the sun. His teeth hadn't seen a dentist in decades, and his fingers were the yellowed stubs of a chain smoker.

What is this place, Vivian? Why were they dragging that girl into the house?

The man's eyes left her face and aimed at the sky as the last long breath escaped his lips. His chest lowered once more and didn't rise again. The blood pooling out of his leg eased off and stopped.

"Okay, now what, Vivian?" Sarah looked around. "I really hate not knowing the details, and I can't keep killing people and expect to just walk away from this one day. You have to offer me more." She got to her feet. "Stake out a cottage. Watch the place. But for what? And now this guy is dead."

A female screamed inside the house. Then another.

"How many people are in there?" Sarah asked aloud.

The woman was either calling the police or waiting for Sarah with a weapon of her own. If the police were coming, they would have her because the gate was closed and electrified. She couldn't jump it without being cut to shit by the barbed wire.

The only option was to wait out here all day or enter the

house and get to the bottom of this task.

She looked down at the body at her feet as an idea sprang to life.

Quickly, she got to work. Once the man's body was placed in the Adirondack chair, to an outsider looking in from at least a couple of dozen feet, he appeared to be sleeping.

Sarah wedged her gun between the man's shoulder blades, completely out of sight, then leaned the chair back to the point where it was almost level with the ground. Hunched over, she dragged the chair occupied by the dead man toward the back of the house.

"He's wounded," she yelled. "He needs help." Then in her most feminine voice, she cried out, "Please help. It was an accident."

Even though the soil was soft, pulling the Adirondack loaded with 160 pounds of dead weight was exerting. The strain weakened her already drained body. She was sure of one thing, though. She would drink water for the first ten minutes when she got inside that house.

The chair caught on a rock, ceasing her progress. She turned back, lifted the chair up on one leg, and pulled, clearing the rock. Then she dragged on until she reached the back of the wooden deck, her eyes on the back door the entire way.

"Help," she called as she settled the chair back slowly so as not to spill the dead body from it. "Anyone?"

Through the rear sliding door, the kitchen was empty. A hallway led from there until it ended at the house's front door. It was also empty. She looked up to see both windows on the second floor were curtained and closed.

She retrieved her weapon from behind the dead man and

stepped onto the deck, her heart aflutter with the adrenaline still pumping throughout her.

To remain calm, she took deep, relaxing breaths. The bad part of taking a house is not having backup. The other bad part was having no clue where her enemy was or how much firepower they carried. The worst part was having no idea why she was here in the first place and having no other option but to move forward, enter the house, see for herself, and then it would be over. Then she could get some water.

Damn that whiskey.

She thought she heard Vivian second that but was sure Vivian wasn't interested in disrespecting her at the moment. The last thing they needed was a family fight on the back porch of this house. Vivian could throw debilitating punches that knocked Sarah unconscious, and all Sarah could do was rant and rave at her.

So not fair ...

The back door eased open without effort. The moment she stepped inside, a smell assaulted her. Then voices. Many of them. All coming from below.

The smell reminded her of bad milk mixed with broken eggs left to rot. It was so bad she leaned on the counter for support.

What the hell is that?

Whatever it was might be why Vivian hadn't explained what she would find here. She was starting to wonder if she even wanted to know.

Her arms were exhausted from pulling a dead body to the back deck and weakened from holding the gun out in front of her. She took a deep breath of outside air and held it as she traversed the kitchen and quietly headed down the hall.

The walls were filthy. The floor appeared to have never been swept. Near the front of the house, she crouched by a wall and peered around the corner slowly. A living room with no one in it.

Where did the woman go?

The living room wasn't being used as a living room. The tenants had turned it into some kind of video production studio. By the dirty front window, a large camera rested on a tripod. In front of it was a lounge couch, and behind that, a bed. Various props—ropes, handcuffs, and a variety of adult toys—lay strewn about out of sight of the camera. A desk with two laptops sat to the side, up against the wall. She gathered quickly that the computers were probably for webcams and the voices downstairs were the stars of the show.

A porn company, Vivian? Webcams? Really?

Vivian's voice reminded her of the electrified fence and the iron gate. The security. The man with a rifle was willing to murder an intruder without a single word or warning uttered.

There's more, Vivian whispered. *Get downstairs.*

Sarah trembled at the thought of what was downstairs. Images of Elmore Ackerman came to mind, and she shuddered again. The man who had held her and Drake hostage after helping them escape the police. It had been a house like this, just north of Toronto. Elmore had cages built in the basement for his victims.

And where's that fucking woman?

At the top of the stairs that led to the basement, Sarah stopped as a voice boomed up from the lower depths of the house.

"Coming down to play?" a female called.

"Not sure if I have time today," Sarah said.

"Sure, you do. Isn't that why you came alone?"

"Backup's on its way," Sarah said. The woman's name popped into Sarah's consciousness. "They'll be here soon, Belinda."

"How do you know my name?" Belinda shouted. "And why did you have to kill my Joel?" Her voice cracked as she spoke Joel's name.

Sarah checked over her shoulder. It felt like no one else was on this floor, and so far, she had detected nothing from the upper floors.

With the basement door fully open, she stared down the steps to a concrete floor. The smell was different than in the kitchen. This was more human. The scent of sweat, urine, and feces wafted up the stairs. It was like breathing the odor of roses compared to whatever was in the kitchen.

"We've been tracking your movements for some time, Belinda," Sarah said in an attempt to sound like the authorities. "It's over. That girl you dragged in the house was your last one." She waited to let her words sink in. "Joel died as he should have. In the dirt like the piece of shit he was."

"Joel wasn't a piece of shit!" Belinda screamed, her voice taking on a high-pitched psychotic quality. "I will kill them all before you take them from me."

Them?

"Help us," someone else shouted from the basement.

The distinctive sound of knuckles whacking flesh and then a grunt of pain followed the plea. Asking for help would get a shot in the mouth. Whoever was down there was afraid of Belinda. She had some kind of control over them. Or they were subdued in some way?

Someone sobbed as they tried to breathe through their tears. Sarah barely heard someone else whisper, "Shut up."

"I'm coming down," Sarah said.

She crouched to the floor and eased forward, ready to yank her head back as she peeked into the basement.

Belinda sat in a chair in between two beds that resembled hospital gurneys. Between her legs, on the floor in front of her, was the girl from the car Sarah saw being dragged into the house. Belinda had a large, rounded blade resting against the girl's throat.

"Come on down," Belinda said. "Watch as I slit this whore's throat from ear to ear."

Females occupied both hospital gurneys in different states of wretchedness. The girl on the right was missing a foot, the stump wrapped in bloody gauze. Her right hand had bandages covering what looked like fingers that had been taken off. Large, grotesque stitches—the kind found on patients of mad doctors—covered most of the visible skin. Her eyes were closed. Sarah couldn't tell whether she was dead or asleep.

The other bed was occupied by a girl who was awake, her eyes frantic and wild. She wasn't as beat up but was tied to the bed. Fresh blood ran from the corner of her mouth, evidently, the one Belinda punched. There was something wrong with her hands and feet, though. Like the skin was yellowed only in those areas. Could she have a whole-body bruise? Or is a liver problem causing the jaundiced look? If so, what exempted her face from blemish?

There was no gun in sight. Maybe Joel had the only gun in the house. Who knew when their captives would rise up and revolt? Better to keep the guns limited and out of sight.

The disgust and revulsion that wrapped around Sarah's abdomen tightened and mixed with the smell wafting up from below. She choked back the urge to vomit. She got to her feet and started down the stairs, hunched over so she could watch Belinda as she descended. The last thing she needed was a surprise attacker coming out of the back corner or from under the stairs.

It occurred to Sarah that the voice she heard before falling asleep in the Adirondack chair outside must've come from the girl with the clear face and yellowed appendages. Maybe Sarah should have broken into the house then and waited down here for Belinda and Joel to arrive home to a surprise.

With four stairs left to descend, Sarah stopped. What she hadn't seen—couldn't have seen from the top of the stairs— were the two girls tied up in the far corner, legs splayed out on the floor.

Bile rose in the back of her throat.

Oh, Vivian, no ...

She wondered why Vivian would bring her here and not simply supply the address to the police. Only Vivian knew what motivated Vivian, and Sarah was sure there was a reason—a greater reason. Moments like this made her wonder if she could go on living in the same world as people like Belinda and Joel. Even in the face of the repulsive abuse that huddled in the corner of the basement, Sarah took another step forward. Then another, wondering from where she drew the strength.

Oh, please, God, Sarah thought. *Have mercy on them. Please allow them to be dead already.*

"What's the matter?" Belinda asked. "Frightened by our dolls? Is that why you killed Joel? Now this whore will not live long enough to be our plaything. Sad, really."

Sarah raised the gun and aimed it through watering eyes at Belinda from ten feet away. Belinda was mostly hidden behind the crying young girl. The odds of hitting Belinda were extremely low.

Vivian, you controlled my hand with Vanessa on the tower. Control it now. Make a sure shot. Don't fucking miss.

"Go ahead," Belinda shouted. "Shoot. But I'll take this one with me."

Belinda's arm moved.

Sarah's hand numbed, and the gun wavered.

The blade started across the tender flesh of the girl's neck.

The gun righted itself and locked into position.

Sarah watched as Vivian squeezed her finger on the trigger, the barrel holding true.

Then the screaming really started.

Chapter 12

Detective Timothy Simmons entered his office and dropped into his chair, exhausted. It spun in a half circle until he faced out the window. Outside, the busy street was littered with lunch traffic, people walking left and right without a care about the criminals amongst them. Cars scurried by, racing around illegally parked couriers, horns blaring, drivers shouting.

Tim ran a hand through his hair. It had been a long night interviewing Aaron Stevens, but in the end, they got nowhere, no closer to locating Sarah. Aaron knew nothing. The last he'd seen Sarah was in California. She called and asked for a favor. He moved her car to a rendezvous point. That was it. That was all he knew. And there was nothing illegal about that.

Between interviews, Tim had taken a break to pull Aaron's file and to suck back a coffee with four painkillers for his aching, broken hand. Reading the file, he discovered Aaron's history with Detective Folley regarding Aaron's missing sister, Joanne Stevens. Maybe it was Aaron's vigilante side that first attracted Sarah to him.

Aaron's case was unusual. He had not only investigated his sister's disappearance on his own, but he also ended up being kidnapped, flown to Greece and shot multiple times in an ancient stone prison called Palamidi.

Aaron, the trained fighter, had balls. But he was stupid, too. Investigating his sister's disappearance could have cost him his life. Aaron would be dead right now if his friends hadn't shown up in Greece to stop his murder. Life wasn't something you left up to luck. Especially someone as calculated and disciplined as Aaron. But he had raced after his sister's killer like a blind rodent wandering aimlessly into its predator's mouth.

Tim rose from his chair and headed for the door. They couldn't hold Aaron. They had nothing on him. His story checked out. They had no leads and no Sarah Roberts.

And Tim's police-issue weapon was still missing.

At the door, his phone rang. He stopped, his hand on the knob. On the third ring, he decided to take the call.

Behind his desk again, he picked up the phone.

"Detective Simmons here."

"Detective," a male voice said softly.

"Who's this?" Tim leaned forward and placed his elbows on the desk.

"Tim Sim. It's been too long."

Tim Sim?

He hadn't been called that in a long time. The play on his name was common in high school and, later on, police college. The people he knew since making detective never called him that.

"Who is this?" he asked again.

"We've met once before."

"And …"

"Look, I'll get to the point. You've got a little mess that needs cleaning up."

"Listen, asshole, I'm going to hang up now. Not interested in what you're selling."

"A lot of people will die if you hang up."

The silence that followed allowed Tim to hear the caller's breathing. A distant memory was surfacing. The voice was recognizable, but he couldn't place it.

"You've got my attention."

"Good."

Papers shuffled on the other end of the line.

"Why is Sarah Roberts in Toronto?"

"No idea."

"Is she of interest to you?"

"What's your stake in this?" Tim asked.

The caller's name was close. An old school friend, a neighbor, an associate. He had to keep him talking.

"I'll ask the questions. That agreeable?"

"This kind of mysterious phone call only happens in the movies. Unless you've recently escaped a rubber room. Are you for real?"

"That was your last question. Understood?"

When he said *understood* in a deeper, more pronounced voice, the caller's name popped into Tim's head.

Toronto City Councilor Marshall Machiavelli.

He had worked closely with Marshall during the last

Toronto mayoral elections. Security detail had been compromised, and detectives without a large caseload were assigned to locate the insiders. Some believed there was an old boys' club that Marshall spearheaded. The media mentioned multiple councilors in the past decade as club members. Harold Hoffenburg, Fletcher Aldrich, and Omar Howe, who represented Hamilton and the Turner brothers, Ruben and Shawn. Ever since Toronto amalgamated and became the GTA, the Greater Toronto Area, the rumors of the old boys' club thrived.

So why is Marshall calling me?

"What have you learned from Sarah's boyfriend, Aaron?" Marshall asked.

"Nothing I'm willing to discuss on this call."

"Are you saying you still have no clue what Sarah is up to?"

"No comment."

"You're lying. You know something."

"How's that?" Tim asked. Then in a snarky, sarcastic voice, he said, "Or am I not allowed to ask *you* anything?"

"We all know who shot Vanessa."

Tim tightened his grip on the phone at the sound of his daughter's name until the plastic case whined under the strain.

"C'mon Tim Sim, I've seen the footage. Sarah Roberts brought a parachute, disguised as a backpack, to the roof of the CN Tower, shot your daughter, and then jumped and disappeared. Suddenly, after your daughter's funeral, you're having a drink with her in the pub where you practically gave her your weapon. If you're not involved, when the disciplinary actions come down the pipe, you're going to have a hard time explaining that. Especially explaining your involvement with The Club." He cleared his throat and coughed into the phone.

The Club?

There was that name again. A horrible place that every cop in the city left alone. They paid their taxes, and no one ever complained about The Club. Ever. Tim knew of several members and a few who visited The Club, but it was always hush-hush.

"Rumor has it Vanessa recently stayed at The Club's warehouse, courtesy of The Club's hospitality. But she left after a few nights. Somehow she escaped their welcoming arms. But we now know how she got out, and it is being dealt with."

Why is he telling me all this?

A thought struck Tim so hard that he winced. To know anything about The Club was to be on the inside. Since Tim was on the *out*side, would he disappear like Officer Mark Hemmings did a week after that Christmas party? Was Marshall telling him this information because, in the end, it really didn't matter what Tim knew as his days were numbered like Vanessa's had been?

Vile anger, a seething fury, rose in a flash and then abated just as quickly. He clenched and unclenched the fist of his free hand. He couldn't deal with this call, the loss of his daughter, and veiled threats from an asshole councilman with anger. He would beat them by staying calm.

"If The Club was responsible for Vanessa wanting to kill herself—" His throat clenched with emotion. He swallowed and tried again. "If they hurt her, I will kill—"

"Easy, easy, Tim Sim. Your anger is misdirected."

Someone knocked on his office door. "I think you need to direct your anger where it matters." They knocked again. Then his doorknob twisted. "It's Sarah Roberts who hurt Vanessa, not The Club. We were kind to her. She enjoyed herself in our presence."

The door opened, and Detective Marina Diner stepped in. She mouthed the words, *you okay?*

"Find Sarah," Marshall said. "End this stupidity. Powerful people need this to be quelled. Consider your career. If you don't end this, walk out of your office now and leave a note behind describing where you want your ashes to be strewn because it all ends in death, Detective Simmons, it all ends in death."

The line went dead. Tim slammed the phone down. Marina flinched.

"What was that all about?" she asked.

"Telemarketer. What's up?"

"You're pale. Your eyes are red, and you look like you just broke out in a sweat. Are you okay?"

"Pain in my hand. No sleep. We haven't found Sarah, and I have to go home now. Nothing is working out, is it, Diner?"

"No, I'm afraid not."

"Why are you here?"

"Came to tell you that we had to let Aaron Stevens go, but we kept the Charger."

"Fine. Fuck him. We'll find Sarah without his help."

Tim got up and stormed past Marina.

"I'm sure we will," she said behind him.

He passed Detective Mason standing outside his office door.

"What are you looking at?" Tim asked.

"Death warmed over. A zombie. You're looking bad, Detective Simmons. Maybe bereavement leave is in order."

Tim turned to face Mason. He never really liked Mason or his strait-laced partner, Diner. And now they hung over this case and his office like he was a suspect.

"What gives you the fucking right to—"

"Detective Simmons!" Diner shouted as she exited his office. "Move along. Go home. Sleep. Don't come back until you're thinking straight."

Doors opened along the corridor. Their colleagues stepped out to watch the fracas.

Tim wouldn't give them the pleasure or the satisfaction of decking Mason. They weren't worth it.

He spun around and strode for the exit. He would be back later in the day, and when he returned, he would investigate The Club. Maybe he'd pay them a visit. Why had his daughter been there? They had to have picked her up for some reason because she would have never gone there voluntarily. Whatever the reason was, what Sarah said made more sense now. When she told him Vanessa feared cremation, he had thought of the consortium, The Club. That was how they dealt with the unfortunates who died under their care. But there was no way Vanessa would know that.

But if she had been there …

It all ends in death, and she didn't want to be cremated.

He was sure it would end in death if they had taken Vanessa there. He suspected what really happened inside the walls of The Club's warehouse. He knew what they did to young, clean, innocent girls and boys.

It looked more and more like this would all end in death.

The Club's or his.

Chapter 13

Sarah's bullet, guided by Vivian, made a clean entry into Belinda's right eye. It left a gaping black hole beside her nose and a large red hole at the back of her head. The arm that had guided the blade across the young girl's throat had faltered, stopped, and slipped to Belinda's lap.

The girl in Belinda's clutches had screamed at the sound of the gun, but the gun's report had drowned most of it out. The girl had also jumped in panic, jerking Belinda's arm away from her enough that as the blade began to cross her flesh, it only nicked a small piece of skin below her jawline. Besides the bruises on her face, being startled, and going out of her mind at the sights in the macabre basement, the girl was physically fine.

"Get up," Sarah said, amazed she could find her voice.

Vivian's numbing of her gun hand wore off as fast as it came on.

The girl was already crawling away from Belinda's body. She clambered to her feet at the stairs and rushed up the steps, only stumbling once.

Without looking back into the corner, Sarah checked Belinda's pulse to ensure she was gone.

"Is she dead?" the girl on the bed asked, her voice weak.

"Looks that way." Sarah scanned the woman's body. Their eyes met. Insanity lingered behind the soft brown eyes of a once beautiful woman. What the woman must've endured down here had changed her forever. This was the kind of thing a team of therapists could listen to in group therapy and then need therapy themselves for having heard it.

"What happened here?" Sarah asked with trepidation, not sure she wanted to hear the truth.

The girl rolled back in the bed until she stared at the basement ceiling. She panted, breathing in and out in gasps now. Between breaths, she tried to speak.

"They kidnapped … us."

Sarah looked around at the filth to determine where the smell was coming from.

"They tortured us, raped us, and dismembered us."

Dismembered?

Sarah's eyes shot to the woman's yellowed hands and feet. Moments before, she thought it was a body bruise or a malfunctioning liver. But now, this close, she saw what was strapped to the woman's limbs.

"They cut those girls up," she jerked toward the corner where the two bodies lay tied to the wall. The two that Sarah hadn't looked back at yet. "And placed their hands and feet on my stumps after removing mine."

Sarah had heard enough. She stumbled away, bumped

Belinda's body, and fell, hitting the basement's concrete floor with a thump as vomit shot from her whiskey-addled stomach.

Oh, Vivian ...

"I'm sorry," the girl continued. "Please. Help me. Get me out of here."

The woman who had run upstairs began screaming. She shouted something incoherent as Sarah vomited again.

Her anger rose with the bile. She understood her path and destiny in a distant part of her consciousness. She always had, but since stopping Armond Stuart in Europe and Elmore Ackerman in Toronto, she had slipped a little. She had grown softer, cooler. Maybe even a little arrogant. Her youthful ways back when she was a newbie at this had kept her alive. She had a mouth on her in those days and an attitude that made her feel invincible. But recently, she had found love with Aaron. As beautiful as love was, it had softened her. She could still love, but to do what she did with Vivian, she needed to pull from the place she used to pull from. She needed to get angrier and deal with people like Joel and Belinda without remorse or worry about consequences. No court of law could ever pass sentencing that made up for what had happened here in this basement.

If that meant Sarah had to go underground, then so be it. Vivian would teach her and keep her safely hidden. But in the end, her *life's* mission was to locate people who broke the law and not only got away with it but never *really* paid for what they did.

These abused women would pay for the rest of their lives if they lived long enough to allow that suffering.

Sarah wept on the cold basement floor as she wiped bile

from the edge of her mouth. Vivian snuck into her consciousness and whispered that she was sorry, but there was no other way. Sarah needed to get back to Toronto to deliver a message. The police were on their way. The girl upstairs had called them.

Then, in a brief flash, Vivian explained what had happened here.

Sarah's stomach clenched again, this time more violently. It made her feel weak, but most of all, it made her feel human. And to be human is to be humane. To be humane meant people like Belinda and Joel didn't deserve life sentences in cushy prisons, meals at set hours, and workout routines. No, to be humane was to rip their heads off for what they had done to these women.

Sarah whispered a small prayer for the girls in the corner as she understood why they looked so horrid now. Their skin had been removed in spots and interchanged with the other's body in a grotesquery of puppetry. Several parts of their bodies were hacked out or off and were used in sexual ways that Sarah didn't even know were possible.

Dolls, Belinda had called them.

The girl on the other bed was dead. She had died that morning, hence the search for another hitchhiker today to replace their dead toy. The horrid stitch job had been Joel's insane search for a demon he claimed had hidden in her flesh. The same demon that forced him to rape her countless times in unimaginable ways.

All this and more came to Sarah through Vivian's unique presence. Sarah didn't want to know anything else; she couldn't stand the thought of it. Her sanity tilted momentarily, leaving Sarah wondering if she would slip into blissful madness. That might be a better alternative than being aware and awake.

She struggled to her feet, weakened by the expelling of her stomach and her physical setbacks before arriving at the house. Once standing, she held the railing by the stairs and waited until her head cleared.

"The police," she licked her lips and swallowed, her throat dry. "The police are coming. You can go home soon." She started up the stairs, then stopped. A glance at Belinda's body created a revolting disgust that she had never felt. She raised the weapon and fired twice into Belinda's face and throat. Then she looked at the woman on the bed.

"I'm sorry." She caught a tear with the back of her wrist as it descended her cheek. "I'm so, so sorry."

She entered the hall at the top of the stairs and turned for the back of the yard. The hitchhiker Belinda and Joel had snatched earlier sat curled up on the floor against the cupboard, sobbing.

"I called ..." She hiccupped. "I called the police."

"Good," Sarah said.

The smell in the kitchen was just as bad as before, but this time, Sarah knew the source, thanks to Vivian. Body parts, feces, and decaying flesh was wrapped in a bag for later disposal. The bag was leaking under the kitchen sink.

"Maybe you should wait outside," Sarah suggested. "Smells better out there."

"I'm not going near him." She pointed at Joel's body in the chair by the back porch.

"He's dead. He can't hurt you. Come on."

Sarah offered a hand, and the girl took it. Outside, she helped the girl onto the grass where she lay out and stared up at the vast blue sky. Then Sarah moved to stand in front of Joel. As with Belinda, Sarah raised Simmons's weapon and emptied it into Joel's dead body.

"There, he can't hurt you ever again. He's not just dead; he's completely dead."

She placed the gun down in front of Joel. After a quick search of his pockets, she located the gate fob, deactivated the electrical fence, and opened the iron gate wide.

Sirens wailed in the distance, leaving little time. She exited the property without looking back, only pausing to grab a tin can that once held corn out of their recycle bin and continued walking.

She left the nightmare behind her. The heat didn't bother her. The lack of water made her stronger. She walked with purpose, the tin can in her hand, and returned to the highway.

According to Vivian, there was a lot to do yet. This was only the beginning, and even though Sarah wasn't too keen on dealing with anything remotely like what she had just witnessed, she was determined to end this her way, the only way she knew how. The old Sarah way.

Wanting to scream, push the memories back, and allow the anger to flow, Sarah walked faster, her energy brimming over.

Moments later, she was running; her teeth clenched as she cried for the lost ones.

"No more," she shouted at the bushes. "No more fucking around!"

Chapter 14

SARAH MADE IT TO Toronto with time to spare. The easiest way was to hike a half hour into the southern tip of Orillia. Soon she came to a hospital and found a cab to take her to the casino.

In front of the casino, she had a pick of which limousine would take her south to Toronto. This time she chose a stretch limo to rest in the back.

Once inside, she had the driver close the window between him and the back, turn off the interior lights, turn the air conditioning up full, and take her to city hall, downtown Toronto. The tiny fridge in the limo was filled with bottles of water. After finishing two bottles, she nursed the third one as her eyes fluttered shut.

Hours later, as the sun leaked behind the distant clouds in the west and an ash-colored sky gave way to darkness, Sarah shuffled along Queen Street toward Nathan Phillips Square, the tin can from the horror house clutched firmly in her hand. They would find Simmons's gun on the ground in front of Joel. Once the serial number was run through the system, Simmons would be contacted. It would lead back to Sarah, and ultimately the death of Joel and Belinda would fall on her head. But that didn't matter anymore. She was happy she killed them.

A memory from the CN Tower surfaced. Sarah had said to Vanessa, *No one has to die*, and Vivian had whispered inside Sarah's head *famous last words*. Sarah wasn't sure what her sister meant at the time, but she knew now and completely agreed. Some people should die. They didn't belong with the rest of civilized society. People like Belinda and Joel weren't contributing members of the human race anymore. She once heard someone say that there were two kinds of people in the world, hammers, and nails. Some people were the hammer, and some were the nail. But then there were people like Joel who *thought* he was a hammer.

This would end soon, Vivian had said. But first, a few small tasks were left. Easy tasks.

Famous last words, eh Vivian?

Easy tasks. It was never easy with Vivian. But that didn't matter anymore, either. Sarah was angry and wanted people to pay more for their actions than ever before.

Groups of people gathered in front of city hall. The buildings were tall and shaped like crescent moons. The unique construction of Toronto's city hall stood out amongst the tall buildings surrounding them in the core of a large, magnificent city. But what came with large cities like this one was crime. A lot of it. Crime on a scale that would keep someone like Sarah in full-time work.

Large tour buses lined Queen Street in front of Nathan Phillips Square. Close to the front of city hall, tents had been erected for some kind of flea market.

Buses emptied as hundreds of tourists headed toward the tents. Somehow, in this throng of people, Sarah was supposed to locate a man named Fletcher Aldrich, Joel's brother, and give him a note. She still had no idea what the tin can in her hand was for, but Vivian said she'd let her know when the time was right.

Sarah started across the concrete walkway, her stomach growling at the smell of a hotdog stand. Since leaving that house, she hadn't thought about food, a shower, or much else.

Meet Fletcher, Vivian had said. *Give him the note.* Then she could call to see if Aaron had been released yet.

Or maybe not.

There was no point in involving him further. She'd call him when whatever she was doing in Toronto was over.

Joel's brother, Fletcher Aldrich, was a Toronto councilman who was supposed to represent his constituents but was involved in something dreadful. His crimes were still being kept from Sarah, but knowing he was Joel's brother, she suspected it had to be terrible.

She had to promise Vivian she wouldn't kill him, though. He was entering the mayoral race this year and was popular among the people. Killing him here tonight ended Sarah's career as a vigilante. Leaving him with the note would be all that was needed.

Sarah stood in the center of the throng while men in suits came and went through the front doors of city hall.

How will I know him? Sarah asked.

She waited but felt nothing from Vivian. Earlier, when

the limo had dropped her off close to where the buses were letting people out, she had walked a couple of blocks down Queen Street until she found a store that sold hair products. After tying up her hair, she bought a baseball cap with a blue jay on the front, and on the back, it said Toronto Blue Jays and something about being winners in 1992-1993.

Disguised as best she could in the short time she had, she waited in the bright lights surrounding the entrance to city hall for Fletcher Aldrich.

Fletcher could be the same kind of man as his brother. Wealth had a way of protecting criminals. But when they fell, they fell the hardest. She had recently read in the *Globe & Mail* newspaper about Helmuth Buxbaum, a millionaire imprisoned for arranging his wife's murder. He died behind bars in 2007. Conrad Black and Garth Drabinsky, both rich men, were jailed for fraud. It didn't matter how wealthy Fletcher was. If he had anything to do with what Joel had been up to, Sarah would find a way to deal with him.

The crowd enlarged around her as she was lost in her thoughts. Now the crowd closed in even more, people pushing and shoving. Someone stepped on someone else's foot, and another bumped someone into a table.

What the hell?

The front doors to city hall were pushed open and held there. An entourage of men filed out.

There he is, Vivian said. *In the long, beige overcoat.*

Sarah had to jump to see over the heads of the people in front of her. It was easy to spot Fletcher. She saw the family resemblance to Joel and was happy she had left the gun behind.

But now, getting close enough to give him the message

was impossible. There was no way, short of making a large commotion, to get out of the throng shoving their way by her. It was like she was stuck in a rock concert crowd after a fire alarm had been pulled, moving upstream with the crowd. It was that or be stampeded and stomped on for trying to go the opposite way.

She jumped up to look over the heads of the crowd. Fletcher's entourage was moving to the side, slightly away from her now, heading toward the street. Sarah moved people out of the way, nudged a path for herself, then jumped again.

She was still no closer.

Use the can.

The can? How?

Then it came to her.

She hunched her shoulders as she held the can out. After a moment, she pulled coins out of her pocket and dropped them into the can, shaking it.

Members of the crowd looked her way and gave her room.

"Spare change?" she said. Then louder, "Can you spare some change?"

In under ten seconds, the crowd, still thick and moving as one, had opened around her like a parting of the sea. She shook the can hard and asked anyone who would look at her if they had spare change. A couple of people tossed quarters in as they moved away. The reaction to someone perceived as homeless disgusted her, but it worked. Vivian had known it would work.

On the move now, she caught up to Fletcher's entourage and was ten feet behind as his team hustled toward cars parked on the street by an underground garage door entrance.

The crowd thinned here, leaving room to pick up her speed even more and reach him in time. She tossed the can aside, the coins rolling out along the concrete.

As they reached their cars, two of the four men ran to the other side to get in while one man stopped to open the door for Fletcher.

Sarah stepped on the back of the leg of the man holding the door, slamming his knee into the concrete with the force of her weight. He squealed at the pain.

Using her forward momentum, she grabbed the startled Fletcher by the collar and spun him around. He lost his balance and dropped to the ground on his back, a poof of air escaping his lips as it was forced from his lungs. In that second, she detected the other two men dropping into the car on the other side, oblivious to what had just happened.

Sarah straddled Fletcher, forcing his arms back.

"What the—" he tried to ask, but Sarah slapped the words out of his mouth.

"I'm so sick of people like your brother," Sarah spat. "Look at you. How could you not know who he was and what he was up to? You're just as bad." Instead of slapping him this time, she clenched her hand into a fist and jabbed at his mouth, splitting his lip against his teeth, blood surfacing instantly.

The other two men had gotten out of the car and were coming around the vehicle now, shouting for her to stop.

Time was out.

"Take this, asshole."

She shoved the note into his breast pocket and slapped it. Then she shot upward, spun in a circle to dislodge the hands reaching for her, and ran for the crowd still milling about the flea market.

Shouts to stop followed her as she got lost in the crowd. Moments later, she exited the thickest part of the crowd and headed for Queen Street, baseball cap in hand, long hair flowing over her shoulders.

Her last job of the night was to walk four blocks north of Queen Street to meet a man at Princess Margaret, Toronto's cancer hospital.

For the first time in a long time, she felt energized. Deliver the note. That was all she had to do.

She delivered the note all right.

Sarah style.

She was back. She was angry.

And it felt good.

Chapter 15

Fletcher Aldrich's bruised ego and fat lip infuriated him more than he thought they could. More than he wanted it to.

"I'm calling the police," the guard across from him said, already pulling out his cell phone.

"Don't." Fletcher stuck his hand out, gently pushing the cell phone down. Then he touched his lip, dabbing at the fattest part. "I'll handle it."

The car was underway, driving south toward the Gardiner Expressway.

Could that have been Sarah Roberts? If so, how did she get to him? How could she know of his involvement?

He had to talk to Marshall.

"Driver, pull over."

The car slowed, then stopped at the curb. A taxi's horn sounded before it sped around the stationary vehicle.

"Get out," Fletcher said.

"Sir?"

"All of you, leave me." He reached into his jacket pocket and retrieved a billfold, tossing a hundred-dollar bill to each man. "Take a cab home. We're done for the night. Meet at the office in the morning."

"But, sir—"

"Go," Fletcher said louder.

The men moved slowly, reluctantly, but got out of the car.

"Drive," Fletcher said when he was in the back seat. Then added, "And close the divider."

Once the window was up, Fletcher dialed Marshall. Before hitting the send button, his phone rang in his hand.

"What?" he answered.

His wife waited for her customary two seconds before answering like she was perpetually eating something and needed to swallow before speaking.

"When are you going to be home, honey? I've got dinner on."

"I'll be home within the hour."

"But you said you'd be home early tonight."

"I got delayed."

The pause again. He almost ended the call.

"Why are you talking like that?" she asked.

"I banged my lip."

"On what?"

"Look, honey, I have to go now. I'll be home soon."

"But dinner is ready, and I—"

He ended the call and dialed Marshall. After two rings, it was answered.

"Marshall?" Fletcher asked.

"Identify yourself."

"Fletcher Aldrich, code 0-4-0-7-1-4."

"Go ahead."

"That girl just attacked me."

"The same girl we're having trouble with?"

"The same. At least, I'm pretty sure it is."

"Where?"

"In front of city hall. As I was about to get in my car."

"Your men didn't stop her? Apprehend her?"

"No."

"Why not?" Marshall asked, his tone deeper, angrier.

"She was too fast."

Fletcher's driver took a hard corner to access a ramp that led onto the elevated highway, tossing Fletcher into the side door.

"That is not good."

"I understand. But why me?" Fletcher rubbed his lip again. It seemed fatter somehow. "How could she even know about my involvement?"

"She doesn't. She's fishing. But her boat will spring a leak soon."

"How soon?" Fletcher asked.

"Go home. The Club is closed today. Only the caretakers are there. Everything's fine. We're fine. Relax and tend to your brother's funeral arrangements."

Staring out the window, he almost didn't catch what Marshall said. They were on the Gardiner heading toward the Don Valley Parkway, the driver revving the engine in the fast lane.

Fletcher pushed the phone into his ear. "What was that about a funeral?"

"Oh, I'm sorry. I thought you would've been the first to know, seeing as you're a Toronto councilor, a public figure."

"Is that sarcasm?" Then, after no response, Fletcher asked, pronouncing each word by itself. "What? Funeral?"

"Your brother's. Joel Aldrich was found shot today."

Fletcher shot forward in his seat. "What?"

"Funny thing is, he was shot with the police weapon registered to Detective Timothy Simmons. The same gun that was stolen from him by the girl we're all looking for."

"Are you saying she stole an officer's gun, went to Orillia, shot my brother, left evidence there to incriminate herself, and then came here to clock me one in the mouth?"

"You don't sound too upset about Joel."

"She did us a favor. We tried to include him in The Club, but he wanted to do his own thing. He was a risk, a liability. Is that bitch of his dead, too?"

"Yes, Belinda is gone."

As the driver slowed with the traffic heading north on the Don Valley Parkway, Fletcher stared out the window. His face reflected back at him off the deeply tinted windows, his lip appearing misshapen.

"Marshall. We have to stop her."

"We will."

"It has to be today."

"Anything else?" Marshall asked.

Fletcher knew he was in no position to order Marshall around. The *anything else* comment was sarcastic, telling Fletcher that Sarah was all he had been dealing with since Vanessa's escape from The Club. They could blame Vanessa for fucking everything up, but she was dead. Once Sarah was removed, operations could go back to normal.

"Call the rest of the board," Marshall said. "Get Harold, Omar, and the Turner brothers on alert. Maybe you should organize a meeting. Get everyone together. Contact all your insiders collectively. Get everyone on the streets looking for this girl. She can't be far, and she takes risks, like trying to get close to you. She'll fuck up. We'll catch her. Then we can finish this."

"How will we finish this?" Fletcher asked.

"As we always do. Another funeral, quieter, though. Then the ovens."

"Has anyone located the black book? We have to get that book back. If it fell into the wrong hands—"

Marshall clicked off.

Fletcher leaned his head back and closed his eyes. The adrenaline had fled his system, leaving behind jellied limbs. He shouldn't have asked about the black book. To most, it was a myth. But in reality, The Club needed a ledger of sorts. They needed to make sure whoever came to The Club and used its services remained quiet and loyal. There were clubs like theirs all over the world. The last thing they needed was for it to fall prey to what happened to the one at Dolphin Square in London. At least Marshall didn't allow the victims to be driven back and forth to the parties like their London counterparts. That was too risky. You paid to get in and participate, but you *had* to participate. That allowed you to leave. The subjects, the victims, never left. Ever. Unless they were in a wooden box or an urn.

Fletcher liked it that way. No loose ends and no blood on his hands—unless he chose to have blood on them. But then that was fun.

He expelled a long breath between his now deformed lips

and got ready to call the board members one by one.

Something nagged at him. Something Sarah had done. Before his men got to him, she had slapped his breast pocket.

He looked down, opened it, and saw a white piece of paper folded up inside. He unfolded it and read the words. Ice coiled up his vertebrae as he shivered.

She wouldn't. She couldn't.

He had to stop her. Joel was different. He was an asshole that tortured women and dismembered them for pleasure. Their deal was he would stay quiet about The Club if Fletcher left him alone to his pleasures. Fletcher had agreed. Joel was too stupid to have any longevity in this torture business. Joel would be caught and would commit suicide in prison, or men Fletcher knew on the inside would finish him and have it look like suicide. Joel was different. Learning of his death at Sarah's hand was a good thing.

But the note said that his father would also die for Fletcher's transgressions, and Fletcher couldn't let that happen. His father had been there for him his whole life. He wouldn't be where he was without his father. The cruel world, or universe, or God, or whatever was out there saw fit to give cancer to his hero of a father. He lay withering and dying, with only one wish left. To see his one good son be elected mayor of Toronto, Fletcher aimed to give him that wish before he died.

Instead of dialing the board members, his nervous fingers brought up the Princess Margaret hospital's number from his contact list.

A recording answered right away. He waited as he went through the prompts, sweat forming on his brow with each long second.

"Turn the car around," he yelled at the driver. "Take me to Princess Margaret Hospital. Now!"

An operator answered the phone.

"Put me through to security, please. I need to speak to the head of security."

"Let me see," the operator said. "That would be—"

"I don't care who it is," he shouted. "This is an emergency. I have evidence of a credible threat to one of the patients." His swollen lip ached as he forced his mouth open to bellow. "Just put me through to security."

The operator didn't respond. There was a click, elevator music, then another click.

"Security here."

"My name is Fletcher Aldrich. I'm a Toronto councilman."

"How can I help you tonight, sir?"

"My father is a patient at your hospital."

"Would you like me to put you through to the front desk so they can help you?"

"No. I do not. Someone is on their way to harm my father."

"I'm sorry, sir. Please explain. How did you come by this information?"

Fletcher understood the process. Even after explaining everything to this rent-a-cop, he would sluggishly go to the fourth floor and check on Fletcher's dad. When he found nothing untoward, he would return his oversized paunch to the chair he currently sat in. Sarah was smarter than any of these people. She didn't give Fletcher this note without the foreknowledge that he would call it in. Sarah was prepared. She would be anticipating security, even the police. By now, his father was probably already dead because he took too long to read the fucking note.

Sorry, Dad ...

"Sir?"

"I have information." Fletcher licked his dry lips. "Of a credible bomb threat. Evacuate the hospital now."

"Excuse me, sir? A bomb threat. Is this a drill?"

"This is not a drill. Empty the hospital as fast as possible. Secure the patients. The bomb is real. Do it now. I'm on my way."

Fletcher hung up as his driver wended his way back onto the Don Valley Parkway, heading south toward the core of Toronto.

"Princess Margaret Hospital," Fletcher yelled again. "And hurry."

He forgot all about calling the rest of the board members.

Chapter 16

The phone woke Tim from a deep, dream-filled sleep. In it, he was screaming at Vanessa, angry that she wasn't coming home. He had wanted to ask what her mother would think but thought that inappropriate as her mother had been dead a long time now.

He rolled in bed, wiped his eyes, distantly wondered what time it was, and reached for the phone.

"Yes," he said, his voice clogged with sleep.

"Get up. Get dressed."

"Diner?"

"We found your gun."

His eyes popped open, and he sat upright. "Where?"

"At the feet of the man who was killed with it."

Lead filled his gut as he dropped back to the pillow, his free forearm came up and rested across his forehead.

"Who?" he asked.

"A man named Joel Aldrich. You might know the last name. Brother to Fletcher Aldrich. Your gun was used to kill Joel's woman, too."

"Oh no …"

"Don't worry. Sarah did the world a favor. If I discovered what was in this house, I probably would've shot them as well, and that's saying a lot coming from me."

"What? That is saying a lot." His sluggish mind was slow, putting his thoughts in order. "Wait, what was in the house?"

"Too horrible to describe. One hitchhiker got away clean, thanks to Sarah. Four others, two dead, two alive but needing mental therapy and physio."

"What?"

"Exactly. Get up. Come to Orillia. Call me when you're on the highway. I'll text the address. You can GPS it."

"Okay. What time is it?"

"Nighttime. Hurry."

Tim dropped the phone to his side.

"What have you gone and done, Sarah?" he asked the empty room. "Better yet, what are you doing?"

Tim swiveled in bed and brought his legs over the edge. He rested his elbows on his thighs and ran his unbroken hand through his hair. Yesterday had taken its toll on him. He'd gotten home and fallen right to sleep. The bedside clock said it was almost ten at night.

Orillia? What the fuck was in Orillia?

He got up, urinated, and got dressed without too much trouble, already used to getting his clothes on with a wounded hand.

His phone rang again.

"Coming. Fuck."

He grabbed it on the fifth ring.

"Yeah?"

"Detective Simmons."

Councilor Marshall Machiavelli again.

"I don't have time for one of our philosophical talks, Marshall. I'm in a hurry."

"Make time."

"Excuse me," Tim said harshly. "The last I checked, you're not my boss."

"True. But you're involved with The Club. I'm aware of the texts you receive each month and what name you supply them. I also know who pays you and how much you get for each text. Do we have an understanding?"

Tim moved to the window and looked down at the parking lot of his apartment building. It still took some getting used to not having Vanessa's music blaring in the other room or a couple of her friends over for a slumber party. The quiet of the apartment made him sad and lonely.

For now, he would listen. He would do his job. And when the ax came down, he would be the one holding it. In addition, he would be more diligent in watching his back. No partner was assigned to him, and he liked it that way. He was on his own, and on his own, he would hurt them. The fact that Marshall was calling him meant he had blood on his hands. Marshall was worried about something.

"I'm listening," Tim said.

"Sarah Roberts is in Toronto."

"You must have the wrong information."

"Excuse me?"

"There has been a shooting near Orillia—"

"I'm aware of that. After she killed Joel and Belinda, she made it back to Toronto and attacked one of my colleagues, Fletcher Aldrich."

"You know a lot for a councilor. Tell me, who's on your payroll?"

"You're not listening." Marshall's voice took on a curt tone.

"I'm listening, and I heard you tell me about Joel and Fletcher. Don't you find it interesting that Sarah targeted this family?"

"There is no need to make connections. I'm passing the information along. Sarah is downtown. Where are you? What are you doing about Sarah? Why isn't she in custody?"

Where am I? Why is he asking that?

"Working on it," Tim said, trying hard to keep his voice even and steady. He had to figure out what was happening before it caught up with him.

"Work harder," Marshall said, his voice a gravelly snarl.

The line clicked off.

"Fuck you," Tim said to the phone.

It rang in his hand.

"Holy shit. What now?" He lifted it to his ear. "What?" he almost shouted.

"Sorry to bother you." It was Niles Mason. "We just got a call. There's been a bomb threat at Princess Margaret Hospital."

"Why call me about that? Call the bomb squad."

"Hospital security called it in and are evacuating now."

"So? And why aren't you in Orillia with Diner?"

"Marina drove up while I stayed behind to finish some paperwork. I'm calling you because Fletcher Aldrich phoned a friend on the force who then contacted me."

"Contacted you for what?" Drawing anything out of Mason was maddening. "Why call you?"

"Fletcher was passed a note from Sarah when she attacked him in front of city hall."

He wanted to ask what the note said, but he took deep, calming breaths instead of losing his cool.

Mason continued, "The note told him that Joel was gone, and the next one to go was Fletcher's father."

"Okay, find the father, find Sarah. Sounds simple."

"The father is dying of cancer at the Princess Margaret Hospital, the same one with the bomb threat. Fletcher seems to think Sarah's on her way there to kill his father."

"What? Then why the bomb threat? Is that Sarah's idea to empty the hospital?"

"Fletcher couldn't think of any other way to keep Sarah out of the hospital."

Tim thought he would lose his mind at that moment because it seemed everyone else was going crazy. "You mean Fletcher called the bomb threat in himself to keep Sarah away from his father?" he asked, his voice short, clipped.

"Looks that way."

"Oh my shit, I'm going to have a coronary."

"Just thought you'd want to join me at the hospital. Let's find Sarah and get the answers we need."

"On my way. I'll meet you there. Back parking lot." He clicked off.

As Tim ran for his car, the text from Diner with the address of a house on a rural route near Orillia popped up on his screen.

"Some other time, Detective Marina Diner, some other

time."

He jumped in his car and sped away, leaving a small black strip of rubber on the road.

Chapter 17

SARAH ENTERED THE HOSPITAL through the main doors of Princess Margaret, baseball cap back in place, hiding her hair. She didn't need to stop at the main desk or check in as she knew where Fletcher's dad was.

Vivian explained that Fletcher and Joel were brothers and part of a terrible group that was the brainchild of their dying father. Meet the father. Offer him toilet paper, not Kleenex, for the tears he would shed, and leave it at that. Sarah was to get into private room 404 and hand him water and a roll of toilet paper, then leave and go rest for the night. That was it.

Confused as she was to the purpose of such a meeting, the task didn't sound too bad.

She got to the elevators, pushed the up button, and waited, turning slightly to see if anyone paid extra attention to her. It was easy to spot the cameras in small black domes suspended from the roof. They had her face on file now.

Evidence of her presence would be recorded.

Hey Vivian, we're cool here, right? No more murder?

The elevator doors opened at the same second an alarm sounded.

Fletcher has called it in. He's read the note.

Security guards emerged from a door by the front nurses' station. One was speaking into a microphone attached to a radio on his hip.

Sarah stepped onto the elevator.

"Ma'am?" security yelled after her.

She pushed the number four and then the close button. The doors closed maddeningly slowly.

"We're shutting down, ma'am …"

The doors shut, and the elevator rose to the fourth floor. The alarm sounded inside the elevator. Then it suddenly stopped as a voice came through a speaker above her.

"We are currently in the process of evacuating the hospital. This is not a drill. Those who can, please move toward the nearest exit and …"

The elevator slowed as the fourth floor approached.

Sarah stepped off the elevator and into chaos. Nurses were running, and doctors were barking orders. Gurneys rushed past her, IV bottles banging against their posts.

What the hell did Fletcher tell the authorities?

A quick scan of the room numbers revealed she was two doors from room 404. She would be in and out just as quickly as any of the other patients.

Traffic in the corridor picked up as rooms were emptied, but the door to 404 remained closed. She sidestepped around a slow-moving man with a cane, moved out of the way of a doctor pushing an elderly patient in a wheelchair, and ran for the second door on her left, hoping it was unlocked.

She grabbed the handle, twisted it, and breathed a sigh of relief as it opened. A quick hop and she was inside, already shutting the door behind her. The room was certainly private, with one old man on a plush hospital bed. Flowers and cards lined the shelf by the window. A large TV hung suspended from the ceiling on thick steel bars. In the far corner, a leather couch had been brought in, so the man's visitors had a comfortable place to lounge. A black mini fridge sat beside that.

To her right, a chair was nestled beside the door. It was the perfect height to wedge under the door handle. Once it was secured and Sarah knew they wouldn't be bothered, she advanced slowly to check the restroom. It was empty.

"Can you tell me what's going on?" the man in the bed asked as he rolled toward her.

"Evacuation," Sarah said.

"Why?" he demanded.

Sarah shrugged before entering the bathroom. She removed the toilet paper from its holder on the wall. When she reentered the room, she located a bottle of water in the mini-fridge by the couch.

"Who are you, young lady, and what are you doing in my room?"

"Shut up, old man."

"Excuse me?" Fletcher's dad tried to get up on his elbows. "Do you know who I am?"

Sarah moved to the side of the bed and examined his condition. His skin had a melted look to it, the elasticity gone over the years it served covering his face. Skin pooled near his ears and around the base of his throat. She attributed much of the extra skin to a man who lived a full life of food and drink and who had withered away from the effects of cancer and chemotherapy.

"Who are you?" he asked, his thin lips parting barely enough to expose a tongue that looked so dry and white that, at first glance, she thought it was covered in sand.

"I'm here to deliver a message."

"Fuck your message," the man said. His false teeth clacked together and stayed that way as he added, "I'll have you killed."

"I see you're delirious, insane, senile, and ridiculously stupid. In your weakened condition, you shouldn't be talking that way to someone who could do you harm without much effort."

"Nurse!" he called, his teeth parting slightly in his attempt to yell the word.

"Here, take this." She held out the roll of toilet paper and the bottle of water. "Your mouth is dry. You need water. And you probably need this toilet paper to wipe the tears away when I tell you I killed Joel today."

His eyes bulged and glazed over. The reddened sclera around his pupils seemed to brighten. He attempted to sit up again, but she pushed him back down.

"I don't know what you started or how you raised that asshole son of yours, but I enjoyed killing Joel."

"You've got"—he swallowed and tried to speak through his anger again—"some nerve coming in here and lying to me like this."

Sarah leaned down until she was almost touching his nose. "I'm not lying. Normally I would be kind and feel sorry for someone in your position. But whatever you've set in motion with your sons has my sister pretty pissed off. I can feel her disgust and revulsion in waves oozing from her now."

"You're crazy." He moved his face away and looked at the door. "Nurse!"

They would be coming soon. Evacuating the hospital meant this room, too. As usual, time was running out, and she didn't want to be stopped at this point. Vivian had more for her to do, much more. Whatever she was chipping away at seemed to work, but it still didn't make much sense to Sarah.

"Get out of my room," the old man said.

"Gladly. I don't want to spend another minute in here with you. But first—" Her hand numbed rapidly. Then just as fast, her arms and upper body. She would've fallen to the floor if she hadn't been leaning into the bed.

Vivian!

With great effort, while Sarah focused hard on fighting Vivian, she unrolled the toilet paper and stuffed a small ball of it into the man's mouth. As he struggled to push it out with his tongue, and Sarah struggled to regain control of her body, her hands uncapped the water and poured it over the toilet paper. Then, as fast as Vivian took over, she let go. The internal struggle stopped instantly, and Sarah passed out, dropping beside the hospital bed to the tiled floor.

What felt like a brief moment later, Sarah stirred to the sound of knocking on a door. She opened her eyes to fully comprehend where she was and what had just happened.

She gasped in shock and got to her feet as the banging on the door intensified. Police sirens roared outside the window.

Fletcher's father stared at the ceiling, his eyes open but seeing nothing. The man on the bed was dead. His mouth was filled with toilet paper, a thin sheet dangling out the side where it rested on his cheek. Water had clogged his throat and poured over the rim of his shriveled lips. The lids of his dead eyes had drawn back into the hollow of his orbital bone, leaving behind the terror of death on his features.

"What have you done, Vivian?" Sarah whispered. "I will follow you to the ends of the earth, but outright murder? We never murder someone unless they deserve it. What is this?"

He deserved it.

More knocking on the door. She heard keys going in and out of the lock. "But I don't know that. This is jail time for me. They have my face on camera. I'm on the fourth floor. I can't jump out the window. I'm done, Vivian." Sarah turned to the chair that held the door closed. It had moved sideways slightly with the relentless banging from the hallway. "When you killed this man, Vivian, as righteous as you say it was, you killed me, too."

In time you will understand.

"No!" she shouted, panic entering her system. She had been used in a way that she never thought possible. Welcoming her sister through this form of channeling had been a new and enjoyable experience. It allowed them to work together more efficiently. But this was something altogether different, horrifying, and wrong.

In time ... Vivian whispered. *Leave now* ...

Like a cloud had enveloped her consciousness, Sarah walked toward the room's door, thinking about toilet paper and how it formed a gelatinous goo when wetted. In the back of the man's throat, as he attempted to swallow it with water, all it did was clog up and remove his ability to breathe. She would have to remember that one if she made it out of this alive.

There was still hope that she would escape this. Vivian seemed to be in control and calm about the entire matter.

Sarah kicked the chair aside and stepped up behind the door, her back to the wall.

It burst open, and two doctors stumbled inside. Now that the door was open wide, the alarm in the corridor was much louder.

"What the …?" one said.

"Holy shit," the other gasped.

Sarah eased around the door and hopped into the hallway. The chaos from earlier had subsided as the patients that could walk on their own, wheelchair and gurney-bound patients, and visitors had mostly been removed.

Fletcher called in a bomb threat, Vivian said.

Stay out of my head! I'm pissed at you right now.

Sorry. Can't. You need me to stay alive. Take the stairs. Go to the basement. Once outside, be ready to duck when I tell you to, or you will be shot and killed. I'm sorry, Sarah, but you will only leave this hospital from the morgue.

Chapter 18

PARKMAN ENTERED THE SWISS Chalet restaurant on Yonge Street and spotted Aaron immediately in a booth in the back corner. He meandered through the restaurant until he stood by the table, looking down at Aaron.

"Well?" Parkman said as he set his briefcase on the floor.

"Well, what?" Aaron said a wide smile on his face.

"I haven't seen you since you took off from California. The least you can do is get up and hug me." Aaron pushed out his chair as Parkman continued, "Welcome me to Canada, fucker."

They embraced, both men slapping the other's back.

Pulling away, Parkman held Aaron's shoulders. "How have you been, man?"

"Good. You?"

"Fine, but this Sarah business has me disturbed." Parkman took his seat and pulled it in close to the table.

"What's going on? When she called, did she mention anything to you? What's she up to?"

Aaron rested on his elbows while he toyed with his new goatee. "Nothing. She called out of the blue and asked for a favor. I got arrested. They interrogated me for over fifteen hours and then let me go."

"What was the favor again?"

Aaron filled him in on everything, including the takedown in the Eaton's Centre garage and how he saw Sarah poke her head out of the stairwell.

"And that was it?" Parkman asked. "No further contact?"

"Nothing since."

The waitress interrupted them. Parkman ordered chicken and a beer. Aaron did the same. When they were alone again, Parkman pulled a folder from the briefcase he had brought.

"Sarah said two things to me before she left for Toronto."

"What's that?" Aaron asked.

"That she was coming to see you. She wanted to talk to you. She missed you and wanted to see if there was anything left between you two. Or something like that."

"Okay," Aaron said. "That's good. There is." His eyes darted away, but before they did, Parkman saw their raw emotion.

"The other thing was a request. Vivian had given her the name Niles Mason."

"Niles rings a bell," Aaron said softly as if trying to recollect where he'd heard the name.

"She asked me to learn everything I could about Niles and the people he lives with and works with. When you called me from custody, I bought a ticket on the next flight, and here I am."

"About Niles," Aaron said, rolling his hand in circles in a carry-on gesture.

"Right. Niles Mason is a detective with the Toronto Police Force."

"That's where I heard the name. Detective Simmons grilled me the most, but I think a woman named Diner asked me questions, too. Niles was her partner."

They stopped talking as the waitress brought their beers. They clinked the necks of the bottles together, then took a swig each.

"Sounds like the same Niles." Parkman looked down at the file in front of him. "Born in the sixties, Niles has had a decent career with the force, making detective only five years ago. Now partnered up with Detective Marina Diner, they have solved numerous cases for homicide and specialize in mispers."

"Mispers?"

"Missing person cases." Parkman used his finger to follow the words on the paper. "Niles is married to Samantha Mason, who, as far as I could tell, is a stay-at-home housewife. They have no kids."

"So what's this got to do with Sarah and what she's here for? Did you find any connections?"

Parkman drank more from his bottle and set it back on the table.

"I have no idea. I looked for blemishes on his record and saw none. This guy is a regular Boy Scout. Fuck, he's so clean they'd make him a Scoutmaster."

"There has to be something," Aaron said. "She wouldn't make you go to that kind of trouble to research a good cop."

"That's what I thought." He drank more, the beer going

down good after the long flight from LAX to Toronto. "Then I realized that maybe she just wants this guy on our radar. So I called a couple of friends of mine on the Toronto Police Force while I was waiting for my flight at LAX."

"And?"

"Sarah's in a lot of trouble. Diner and Mason are the detectives tasked with finding her."

"What kind of trouble?"

"Aaron, brace yourself." Parkman crossed his arms and sat back until Aaron nodded. "Sarah is wanted for murder."

"What?" he shot forward.

"They have the murder weapon with her fingerprints on it, and there were over a dozen witnesses to her pulling the trigger. Some of those witnesses are cops. I'm sorry, Aaron, but Sarah might have gone too far this time. She's been lucky before, but this was cold-blooded murder. Now, Sarah has become the unlucky one. And there's more."

The chicken arrived. They asked for extra chalet sauce and dug in. While eating, Parkman continued to explain what he knew and how Sarah would need a good lawyer. He couldn't see any other way out of this mess.

His phone rang as he washed the last of his meal down with what was left at the bottom of the beer bottle.

"Parkman here," he answered, absently reaching for the toothpicks on the table.

He listened to the officer explain their new findings. His contact finished fast and hung up.

Parkman dropped his phone onto the table and hung his head.

"What?" Aaron asked. "What is it now?"

Parkman met Aaron's eyes. "It's Sarah."

"What? Is she dead?"

"No, nothing like that."

"Then what?"

"She might wish she was, though." He cleared his throat and explained what he had just heard about the house in Orillia and the bomb threat at the hospital that was taking place as they ate.

"Oh no …" Aaron whispered, a distant look on his face.

"Sarah stole a cop's gun and used it to kill those people. Then the attack on a city councilman and his dying father." Parkman shook his head. "Oh, no, is right. Wow, I never thought she'd go this far." He gathered his papers and shoved them into the briefcase. "I feel sick now."

"Me too."

"We have to prepare ourselves. They may shoot on sight."

Aaron looked away before wiping at a tear. "Oh, Sarah. What is going on?"

Parkman flipped the toothpick to the other side of his mouth. "I'm sorry, Aaron, but the harsh reality is that Sarah will spend a few decades in jail if she makes it out of this alive. With politicians involved, they'll ask for the longest sentence. It's one thing to hurt or kill in self-defense when dealing with scum. But to attack a councilman," he paused, swallowed loudly, then added, "that's something altogether different."

The toothpick in his mouth snapped in half.

He reached for another, thanking God for life's little pleasures.

Chapter 19

SARAH RAN DOWN THE stairwell two at a time. When she hit the second floor, hospital patients exiting that stairwell door slowed her down. She mingled with the crowd and continued to descend the stairs until she was out the side door. A large group had gathered across the back parking lot. Others formed close-knit groups of people talking, probably trying to determine what was happening. Many of the patients were sitting, but some remained standing. For a cancer hospital, it surprised her how many were smoking. They had decided to use this drill to catch a puff before bed.

Fire trucks, police cars, and ambulances were scattered about as everyone tried to understand what was happening.

Sarah stayed close to the building after exiting the stairwell door, grateful she made it out of that man's private room without being seen.

I hope you know what you're doing, sis.

Near the back of the building, she followed a woman in her forties who was pushing a wheelchair out into the rear parking area. As soon as she got two blocks from here, she would hail a cab and get to a hotel. She had to think. She needed direction, and Vivian would offer it, or Sarah would leave Toronto. There would be no more murder or killing of sick, defenseless people, no matter what they had done.

Vivian, what happened to the morgue? Sarah asked. *I thought I'd be leaving through the morgue.*

What looked like an unmarked cruiser drove by. She froze, hoping he didn't see her. The car continued, its searchlight bouncing across the cars, reflecting off windshields.

She stepped out between two cars.

"Freeze," a man said.

Sarah stopped, raised her hands about a foot away from her waist, and turned around slowly.

Detective Timothy Simmons.

He leaned against the side of a van about fifteen feet away, a gun aimed at her.

"I asked myself," Simmons said. "Was it pure luck or just good fortune when I saw you walking right toward me?"

"Probably luck."

He pushed off the van and moved a few steps closer.

"Why would you say that?"

"I was going to go the other way to miss the traffic out front."

"Are you armed?" Simmons asked.

Sarah shook her head, keeping her hands raised slightly at the waist.

"Oh, right, you left my gun at the murder scene in

Orillia."

Sarah frowned. "Interesting, since I've been in Toronto all day." Would he buy the lie?

"You think a jury will believe that? I think not."

"And you can place me in Orillia, can you?"

"Of course. You left witnesses. The hitchhiker." He lowered the gun as someone walked by. "Just like you let witnesses watch you shoot my daughter." The gun was back in place, aimed at her.

"Why did you lower the weapon?" Sarah asked. "You're a police officer making an arrest in public. People understand the gun in your hand. They get it."

He shrugged one shoulder, then stepped closer again.

"You lowered it so no one would remember you with a gun pointed at the girl they found dead right here. Am I right?"

He shrugged once more. "Something like that."

"Is that what you think Vanessa would—"

"Don't say her name!" he shouted.

In the light from the parking lot's tall lamps, Sarah saw his tears and knew he cried for his daughter and the decision he had made that tore him apart inside. The decision of whether to shoot her or not weighed on him.

"Don't ever say her name again."

Sarah swiveled her eyes from Tim's face to the parking lot and back to Tim, searching for the unmarked cruiser that had passed moments before.

Tim moved closer. He cocked the weapon.

Really, Vivian? Is this how it ends?

He was too close to duck down and try to run. She'd get hit. There weren't many options. As far as she could tell, people were still filing out of the hospital, but no one was nearby. He could shoot her and disappear in the dark at the back of the parking lot, and not a single person would see a thing.

Nervous sweat covered her back, and her knees hadn't felt wobbly from fear in a long time, but they shook now.

"Okay, Detective. You got me." She brought her wrists together. "Cuff me. Take me in. I'll explain everything."

"I don't think so. You'll never see the inside of a courtroom." He moved to point-blank range. He couldn't miss now unless the gun jammed. "I am going to kill you right here, Sarah Roberts. Then it will be over. This gun is unregistered. The serial number's gone. It'll never be traced to me." She noticed his hands were gloved. "Speak to whoever you want to, Sarah, make your peace, and ask for forgiveness, but I don't think anyone or anything will forgive you."

He raised the gun and aimed it at her forehead.

"Wait!" she yelled. "At least tell me why you're into she-males."

He paused, frowning, then lowered the weapon. "What?"

"You know, ladyboys. Why are you so into them?"

"What the hell are you talking about? You're just wasting time."

She dropped to the ground in an attempt to roll under the car behind her as the gun fired. The loud report forced a scream from her lips as she rolled. Unfortunately, the car was too low to the ground for her to crawl all the way under it.

"Fuck!" she railed against it, smacking the underside with her open hand.

The gun went off again. She hadn't felt the impact of the

bullet. It could have happened when she had dropped to the pavement. In a panic to escape, she rolled out from under the car and bumped into something on the pavement behind her. Heart thudding in her chest, Sarah looked into the dead eyes of Detective Timothy Simmons.

Disbelief enveloped her as she lay there frozen, the detective's blood oozing into her shirt and the top of her pants near the belt line.

"What the hell?" she whispered. "He shot himself?"

As soon as she spoke the words, she knew that someone else had shot Tim in the neck and hip area. Tim's unfired gun was still in his dead hand. His cell phone had popped out of his jacket pocket and tumbled to where it lay under her shoulder now.

Who shot the cop?

Another man stepped out from between two vehicles five down from her. He remained hunched over, moving with stealth as he neared her position. She had allowed the panic of the moment to take over and hadn't gotten up for fear a sniper was out there trying to off people in the parking lot.

"Here," the man said as he tossed something at her.

She caught it in mid-air. A gun, the smell of cordite still issuing from its muzzle.

The weapon that killed Simmons.

The man, shrouded in shadows, turned his face away and started off down the parking lot. Sarah checked the chamber. The gun was empty. A moment ago, it had two bullets, and both were in Simmons's body now.

Suddenly the man turned back around and pulled another gun.

"Really?" Sarah asked. "Doesn't this get old?"

"Freeze!" the man yelled. "Sarah Roberts, you're under arrest. Drop the weapon, or I'll have to shoot."

She flung the weapon away, shock settling over her system as she lay with the dead detective.

Get tougher, Sarah. Like the old days. Shake this off and start running.

Sarah sat up, spun on her butt, and lay back down beside a pickup truck. Before rolling away, she snatched Simmons's cell phone off the pavement and gripped it close to her body.

The man fired, the bullet nicking the concrete where her face had been a second before. Only a foot had separated her from an entry wound.

"Stay where you are, Sarah," the man yelled.

His footfalls reached her as he ran toward her position. She rolled under the pickup, waited until he rounded the back of the vehicle, then rolled out the other side. Jumping to her feet, she flung the baseball cap behind her to make a scuffling noise distraction and ran for the hospital, hoping she didn't get a bullet in the back for her efforts.

Bobbing and weaving between vehicles, Sarah ran as if a pack of salivating Rottweilers were on her heels. She chanced a look over her shoulder, but the man was gone. No one was chasing her, and no one was pointing a weapon at her.

The door she had exited not ten minutes ago was clear of people. She rushed inside and started down the stairs.

The nightmare wasn't over. It was just beginning.

"Hey!" a hospital security guard shouted from one stair level above her. "You can't go down there," he shouted.

His heavy steps echoed down after her.

She descended the stairs toward the morgue—Vivian's

prophecy—knowing that Simmons was dead and the gun that killed him was covered with her fingerprints. Whoever that man was in the parking lot knew she would be there. That person knew Simmons was looking for her. They also had an agenda, and that agenda was to execute Simmons.

What they didn't count on was Sarah getting away. What they won't count on is Sarah coming back to continue killing in the name of what was right.

That or die trying.

The guard chased her down the stairs. She slammed a door shut, then shoved a chair behind it before racing down a hallway going deeper into the bowels of the cancer hospital.

Chapter 20

IN THE QUIET BASEMENT of the Princess Margaret Hospital, empty of people due to the evacuation, Sarah checked doors along the corridor. The alarm had silenced. Other than the recently deceased, this area was vacant. She was two hallways from the guard who chased her down the stairs. Whether he got through the blocked door or not, she wasn't sure. But one thing she was sure of, they were coming. The guard would report her. The man from the parking lot—Simmons's murderer—would come for her, too. Locating an exit and simply walking out wasn't looking good. She had to find a place to hide until normal hospital activity resumed.

But where?

A room on the right was bathed in a purple, fluorescent light that reminded her of a nightclub. She had a brief moment where she wondered what that was for, but Vivian whispered something to her about sanitization and germs.

Sarah frowned and kept moving down the hallway.

A door banged in a distant corridor. Voices floated through the corridor coming her way. Someone said the word *girl* and *chased her*.

Vivian, a temporary hiding place would help.

Sarah ran another dozen feet and turned into a cavernous room with what looked like three stainless-steel shelves on wheels in the shape of beds.

Autopsy room? Embalming room?

She wasn't sure, but maybe the embalming happened after the dead left the hospital at a funeral home.

The wall to her left was covered with steel doors the size of mini fridge doors. They had large numbers on the doors and small circular temperature gauges that, upon closer inspection, said the inside was about three degrees Celsius or thirty-seven Fahrenheit.

Cold storage. Dead bodies.

Another door banged in the corridor, closer this time. They were coming, and she had to hide unless she was willing to try to explain everything away, which probably wouldn't be very effective.

"No way," Sarah said to the wall of steel doors.

She glanced over her shoulder at the opening to the room. Someone was coming. Many someones. And they were close.

"Shit."

She opened a door nearest the far wall. A soft smell of death wafted out as the tagged feet of a corpse came into view.

She jammed that door closed and checked another one. Then another, gasping for breath as the smells infused the air with its particular toxins.

Footsteps were closer.

The next door was waist high. When she opened it and discovered it to be empty, the odor of disinfectant hitting her nose, she jammed Simmons's cell phone in her back pocket and dove inside, head first. Once inside, she used her foot to close the door as far as she could without locking herself in.

A thin strip of light kept her from absolute darkness and losing her mind. How much oxygen would one of these things offer? How long could she stay in here, huddled up against the cold? How long could a person handle a few degrees above freezing?

The voices were in the room now.

She shivered with a full-body shake but bit down on the following moan. Every part of her skin that touched the inner walls of the cold storage unit felt like it rested on ice.

She would wait until the voices disappeared. Once they were gone, she would kick the door open and nonchalantly leave this place. She hated hospitals, as a rule. Only stayed in them if absolutely needed. To be stuck in one, and not just stuck, hiding in the morgue, was making her sick.

Add to that how bad this trip to Toronto had turned out to be. What would Aaron think of her now? Sure, come to Toronto, meet with Aaron, chat, and work things out. Instead, she was wanted for murder and had set Aaron up to be arrested in a violent takedown.

The perils of being my boyfriend.

Maybe that was what the message was here. Maybe she shouldn't be attached. Perhaps someone in Sarah's line of work was destined to be single.

Parkman came to mind. She loved him in a different way,

and yet he seemed to make it around her just fine. So maybe Aaron could, too?

She hoped so. That is, if Aaron wanted to be around her. Sarah wanted this life, needed it. She wanted to make things better wherever she could. It was in her soul, belief system, and will to fight. But Aaron just wanted her without the other shit. That was why he left California. That was why he left her.

This might have been a hopeless trip. As the shakes took over and her body fought the frigid temperatures inside cold storage, it occurred to her that they were probably done as a couple.

The light near her feet dimmed and then brightened again. Someone was leaning on the door. She had no defense. If they opened the coffin-sized chamber, they could shoot her and close the door behind them, leaving it closed for a few weeks. Then commit her to the crematorium. No one would ever find her.

That's how it's done, Vivian whispered.

The shadow was at the door again.

"Excuse me, Doctor?" a man said. "Are these doors supposed to be open?"

"No, Officer," another man said.

The light by her feet disappeared as the cold storage door closed and locked from the outside.

"Oh shit," Sarah whispered.

There was no inside release lever. Until someone came and opened the door to let her out, she was stuck inside a cold storage chamber in the basement morgue at the Princess Margaret Cancer Hospital.

Her breath caught in her throat. She broke out in a full-body sweat even though the inside of the pitch-black chamber suddenly got colder.

Then she was panting like she had run a hundred-meter dash. Her heart pounded like a caged animal, angry at the cage that confined it. Her bladder urged release as Sarah fought to control her panic. With each gasp of air, she wondered how much oxygen was left while wondering what cold storage unit she was in.

She hadn't read the number on the outside of the door. She had no idea what chamber she was in on a wall littered with doors.

"Oh shit, oh shit, oh shit …"

Chapter 21

Outside the restaurant, Parkman asked Aaron if he wanted to join him for a digestivo before he headed to his hotel room.

"Sounds good to me," Aaron said.

They walked north on Yonge Street until they found a bar where the music wasn't too loud. Aaron located a table while Parkman went and ordered two Johnny Walkers.

Once seated, Parkman nudged his briefcase up against the wall beside the table and took a large drink from his glass.

"So I got to thinking," he said. "If researching Niles Mason gave me nothing, maybe Sarah wanted me to go deeper. So I looked into his partner, Marina Diner."

Aaron set his glass down and stared across the table at Parkman. "What did you find?"

"She's even cleaner than Niles, and that's saying

something because you can't get cleaner than Niles."

Aaron drank half his whiskey in one gulp.

"Is there something else in that file except clean cops?" Aaron asked.

"There is one thing."

"What's that?"

"There's a cop missing. Officer Mark Hemmings has been missing since just after last Christmas."

"How is that connected?"

"Hemmings was Mason's old partner."

"Okay. Fluke coincidence since Sarah asked you to look into Niles, or do you think Niles has something to do with Hemmings's disappearance?"

Parkman popped another toothpick from his stash into his mouth, played with it momentarily, then drank the rest of his whiskey.

"If Niles had anything to do with it, he's damn good. The night Hemmings was reported missing, Niles was on vacation. I checked where he went and found pictures of Cancun and the Mayan ruins on his Facebook timeline. Niles wasn't even in the country when Hemmings disappeared."

"So it wasn't Niles Mason?"

"It wasn't Niles, but there's something. Otherwise, Sarah wouldn't have asked me to look up—" Parkman's cell phone buzzed, notifying him he'd received a text.

He looked down at it.

"That's weird," he said.

"What?" Aaron asked.

"I just got a text that says, and I quote, 'I'm in the cancer hospital morgue. I'm freezing. Hurry.' And it's from a number that I don't know."

"That is weird."

Parkman tilted his head in thought and stared at Aaron through half-lidded eyes. "You don't think it's Sarah, do you?"

"Why wouldn't she use her own cell?"

Parkman shrugged as he looked down at his phone and reread the text. "Not sure. I'll text back and ask."

After typing his question back, he headed to the bar for two more whiskeys. By the time he retook his seat, his phone buzzed again.

"Listen to this," Parkman said. Aaron leaned closer, already half-done his beverage. His eyes were already swimming. "It says, 'Vineyard. Santa Rosa. Gun. Almost shot you. Come now or when I get out, I will shoot you for this. Hurry. Freezing my shit off.'" Parkman met Aaron's gaze. "That's Sarah."

"Then we have to go. Now."

"Where's the cancer hospital?" Parkman asked, already jumping out of his chair. He shot back the rest of his drink, and Aaron did the same.

"Don't know."

Aaron ran for the bar and tossed a couple of twenties on the counter.

"Hey, barkeep? Where's the cancer hospital?"

"Princess Margaret is the cancer hospital," the bartender said, a towel and a glass in his hand.

"Where's that?"

The bartender frowned and pointed out the window. "That way."

"Thanks, you've been a great help," Aaron said sarcastically.

Parkman grabbed Aaron's arm and said, "C'mon. We don't need to know where it is."

They headed for the doors. Clearly, Aaron didn't understand how they would get there if they didn't need to know where they were going.

"But how?" Aaron started. "I don't get it, Parkman. And I don't drink whiskey too often. I don't feel so good. That was a lot of—"

"I know, Aaron. Just come on." Parkman shot a hand out to hail a cab. A taxi did a U-turn and pulled up alongside them.

Once inside, the driver asked them where they wanted to go as Aaron slumped in the seat, leaning his face against the window.

"Take us to the Princess Margaret Cancer Hospital," Parkman said.

"Got it."

The driver watched his mirrors momentarily, waited until a few cars had passed, then did another U-turn and headed south on Yonge Street.

Parkman's cell buzzed again. He checked the message.

"She wants to know if I'm coming."

He typed back that they were on their way.

"I told her we were both coming. She hasn't responded." Parkman looked up from his phone. Aaron stared out the window as if watching the people on the busy sidewalks at this hour. "Did you hear me?"

"Yeah. Just thinking about Sarah and this cycle of always going in after her."

"Just like California, eh?"

"Just like California. And all the other times."

"You okay to do this?"

"That's what I was thinking about." Aaron turned to address Parkman.

"And?"

"And I'm excited to step up and be there for her. I let her down in California. I let myself down. When I pulled away, Sarah was all I could think about. I won't do that again. I owe her. I owe her big. It's funny how this situation has been put in front of me. I've been given a chance to come for her, to help her, and I won't fuck that chance up. I'm in all the way, Parkman. That is if she'll have me."

Parkman smiled. "I'm pretty sure she'll have you. But don't tell me all that stuff. Tell it to her."

"I will, I will. As soon as we save her, I will."

Chapter 22

THE TAXI DROPPED THEM off on the street in front of the hospital. Groups of people mingled outside in various states of dress. Fire trucks, police cars, and several other emergency vehicles, their lights piercing the night, were parked in a jumble surrounding the hospital. If there was a spot a vehicle could be parked, an emergency vehicle filled that spot.

"What the hell happened here tonight?" Parkman asked, taking it all in.

Aaron responded by shaking his head.

"Okay," Parkman said as he placed a hand on Aaron's shoulder. "We have to get inside somehow and make it to the morgue. If they're in some kind of lockdown, this could be difficult. I'm relying on you."

"I'm there. Whatever you need."

"Follow my lead then."

Parkman started off with Aaron following. He led Aaron

through a throng of people talking about another patient. A different group of people was debating why the hospital was evacuated.

He stopped by that group.

"Excuse me," Parkman said. "Can anyone tell me who's in charge here?" He flipped open his private detective badge and shut it just as quickly. "Just point them out to me."

One of their group, a man in track pants and an '80s Metallica shirt, pointed at the front doors as a group of about eight men emerged from inside the well-lit building.

"Those guys look like your best bet, buddy," he said in a helpful Canadian way like he was ecstatic the investigator asked him instead of anyone else. "Otherwise, try any police officer in blue. That might help, eh."

"Okay, eh," Parkman said, trying to sound Canadian. "Thank you. You've been very kind."

He started for the men who had stopped on the front steps. The group consisted of two firemen, two police officers, and four men in suits. They stood just outside the front doors, engaged in a discussion about something. As Parkman drew closer, it sounded like the men were debating whether or not to allow everyone back inside.

Parkman nudged Aaron to stay on his heels as he attempted to get close enough to eavesdrop.

"She's still in there somewhere," one of the cops said.

"We understand," an older man in a suit said. "But I can't have all my patients outside like this. If the bomb threat is over, I'm sending everyone back inside."

"Sir, I'm asking for a little more time," a middle-aged man in a suit with his back to Parkman said. "My men will find her. She killed a patient and shot a detective in the parking lot. She was last seen entering the hospital; no one has seen her leave. How can I make myself more clear? This takes priority over patients getting back in bed."

"You have a job to do, Detective Mason," the older man replied. Aaron nudged Parkman. They looked at each other, eyebrows raised. "And I have a job to do, too. Find your criminals on your own time. I will handle my patients as I see fit. You won't be the one answering questions before the board next week if something happens to any of these people. I will be."

"Fine. It's your hospital."

The men dispersed. Detective Niles Mason walked right by Parkman and Aaron without a second look. He had pulled out his phone and was already speaking into it.

"I've secured both murder scenes." He paused. Just before he got out of earshot, he said, "Yes, I'm waiting for the team to take over the scenes as we speak."

Then he disappeared around a corner.

"What the hell was that?" Aaron asked.

"Bomb threat? A patient and a detective were killed? What's surprising me is that we got close enough to hear all that just when we needed to."

Aaron frowned in his semi-drunken state. "That's lucky, eh?" he said.

People were heading toward the doors in groups. Men in white coats directed them to different doors. It would probably take them an hour to get everyone back to their proper floors and settled into their routines. The perfect time to extricate Sarah was during this shuffle of bodies throughout the hospital.

With Parkman in the lead, they quickly mixed in with a

group entering through the front and headed toward a square map of the building on the wall. The morgue was located two floors below them. After memorizing the route, Parkman headed down the corridor until he saw an exit sign that led to a stairwell. Aaron stayed so close that he bumped into him twice.

The stairwell door opened easily, and once they were safely inside the stairs, he stopped and addressed Aaron.

"Okay, if we encounter resistance of any kind—"

"I'll bust 'em up."

"No, Aaron. I have a plan. Busting people up is our last option."

Aaron nodded and looked at the floor. Parkman could tell the alcohol was affecting him, but he could also see that he wanted to help and would do anything to extricate Sarah safely.

"We have been asked to identify a body."

"We have?" Aaron looked up.

"Yes, Aaron, we have, hypothetically."

"Oh, right. Of course."

"We need to identify a body, and we have to do this in the morgue."

"Got it."

"When I get whoever is down there to open the cold storage—" He stopped talking as three doctors, and one nurse were coming up the stairs from the floor below.

He stepped to the side and let them pass, offering a half smile. The men didn't look their way, but the nurse nodded at them.

Moments later, they were gone.

"As I was saying," Parkman whispered close to Aaron's

ear. "When they open the units and Sarah pops out, I might need you to hold the guy down or do something fancy to put him to sleep."

"Put him to sleep." Aaron nodded exaggeratedly, like he was looking at the ceiling, the floor, then back to the ceiling again. "Easy. I can do that. Next."

Parkman stepped back and assessed Aaron. "Just follow my lead."

"Aye, aye, Captain. Anything for my Sarah."

Parkman half expected a salute.

They descended the stairs and opened the door to the floor where the morgue was. Stealing along the corridor, Parkman softened his footfalls and stayed close to the wall.

A door opened at the other end of the hallway, and five men spilled out, talking about how they couldn't believe they missed her.

"I'll go up and review the cameras," the uniformed security guard said as they neared Parkman and Aaron.

Parkman assessed them quickly. Two security guards, one official in a suit, and two doctors or morticians.

"Right," one of the doctors said. "We'll be down here if she turns up again."

The doctors entered a room on their left and disappeared.

"Come on," Parkman whispered. "Don't forget to follow my lead."

The trio of hospital authorities noticed them a second later.

"Can we help you?" one of the guards said, his voice loud and commanding. "You can't be down here. This is a restricted area."

Parkman pulled his private detective ID, flipped it open,

then slammed it shut.

"Name's Parkman. Here for two reasons. One, through my contact, Detective Niles Mason with the Toronto Police, I'm here looking for a woman named Sarah Roberts." Niles was on sight actively searching for Sarah, so dropping his name made sense.

"So are we," the guard said, the trio still walking toward them. "Niles is upstairs looking."

"We just thought we'd join the search down here."

The men slowed as they reached each other.

"Why does the guy behind you smell like booze?" The guard gestured at Aaron. "Who is he?"

"That's the second reason I'm here. Working a case Sarah's involved with. He's the family of a deceased. He arrived just as the hospital was being evacuated for the bomb threat to do a positive ID on a body in the morgue. He's having a rough time of it, so I thought it best for him to do it now while he's still swimming a little."

A palpable hush fell over them as they stood in the presence of a mourner. The guard edged forward and touched Aaron's shoulder.

"Sorry for your loss," he said. "We'll get her, sir, we'll get her."

Aaron nodded. Then he wiped his eyes as if he was about to cry.

Where the hell did that come from? Parkman thought. *Nice performance.*

"Carry on, boys," the guard said as he passed them. The other men followed the guard until they disappeared behind the door Parkman and Aaron had just come through.

"Well done, Aaron," he whispered. "But we're not out of

the woods yet." They started toward the morgue coming up on the right. "Two doctors are in there, and that guard said he was heading up to review the cameras." He stopped by the open door, still out of sight of the inside of the room where the doctors had gone. "If they see where Sarah went or didn't go, they'll be back within five, maybe ten minutes. We need to find her and get out of here as soon as we can." Aaron nodded. "You ready?" Parkman asked. Aaron nodded again. "Good. Here goes."

Parkman turned the corner and entered the room where the cold storage wall, with its small square doors, gave him the chills. Sarah was in one of them and hadn't offered the location number. Not only that, she hadn't texted in quite a while. Had the cold gotten to her? Was she unconscious? Or did the phone's battery die?

"What are you doing here?" the heavyset doctor on the right asked. "This is a secure facility."

He stood by an open cold storage door, the body of an emaciated female corpse about to be zipped up on the slab in front of him.

"I'm Detective Parkman. This is Aaron Roberts. We're here to do a positive ID on a body."

The morticians looked at each other, then back at Parkman.

"Where's the paperwork?" The man bent to zip up the bag, slid the body back inside, and shut the door. "There must've been a mistake."

Parkman stepped closer. He detected Aaron fanning out toward the other doctor.

"What kind of mistake?" Parkman asked.

"There's no one here by the name of Roberts."

"Ahh, but that's where I think you're wrong," Parkman said, waving a finger back and forth as if speaking to a delinquent schoolboy. "There is a Roberts body here, but we hope she's still alive."

When the doctors exchanged an odd glance between them, Aaron stepped in behind the one closest to him. He wrapped his arms around the doctor's neck and lifted him up and backward. The doctor's arms flailed wildly, and he gasped as his air was cut off.

"Hey!" the other man shouted, taking two large steps toward Aaron.

But Parkman was already moving. He timed it and realized he couldn't get to the doctor fast enough, so he stuck his foot out. The doctor's shin connected with Parkman's ankle. He hated to do it, but they needed to extricate Sarah as soon as possible and at any cost.

The doctor tumbled forward and hit the side of his head on the stainless steel edge of an autopsy table. He crumpled to the floor unconscious. At that moment, Aaron let go of the other man, letting him fall gently beside his coworker.

"There," Aaron said. "Two doctors asleeping." He met Parkman's eyes. "Nice footwork, Parkman. I really like the mad dash, and the foot stuck out like so." He balanced on one foot, trying to mimic Parkman but looking like a man pretending to walk on a tightrope.

"Fuck off, Aaron. Stop screwing around and help me find Sarah. Besides, that was a very lucky hit. I did not think he'd be knocked unconscious."

Parkman wasn't sure he liked the drunk version of Aaron too much. At least not when they needed to be serious.

But he did put the doctor to sleep better than I did.

The man who had hit the table was bleeding slightly. Parkman didn't take the time to scan for cameras in this room as it was too late for that now.

Aaron opened and closed the square doors at his end of the wall while Parkman worked the other end. Almost halfway, he had a fleeting fear that Sarah was in another room. Or worse, another hospital.

Then Aaron opened a door and stepped back.

"Got her," he said.

He eased the slab out, and sure enough, there was Sarah Roberts.

She was certainly frozen, her pale hands on her chest like she'd been dressed and prepared for her coffin. A cell phone was clasped in her grip. She looked so cold it almost appeared as if it had snowed little white crystals onto her clothes.

Her eyes opened, then eased shut.

"Get. Me. Out. Of. Here," she said, barely moving her lips. "Now!" That word came from a deeper part of her throat.

"Aaron, grab the doctor's jackets. We'll need them."

As Aaron disrobed the doctors, Parkman ran to the other corner of the room and unlocked the wheels on a gurney. He swung it around and pushed it until it was beside Sarah.

Aaron slipped into a white lab coat and extended the other one to Parkman. He put it on and nodded for Aaron to grab her feet.

While they prepared, Sarah started to visibly shiver. Parkman thought he heard her teeth chattering.

A door smacked open and slammed shut from down the corridor somewhere.

"We're running out of time," Parkman whispered. "Hurry."

On the count of two, Parkman at Sarah's shoulders, Aaron holding her ankles, they lifted her and gently settled her onto the stretcher.

Footsteps approached. There was no time to hide the doctors.

Parkman swung a white sheet over Sarah's body, covering her face. He leaned down to her ear and whispered, "Don't move the blanket. Don't even breathe."

He thought he heard her mumble a reply but was already standing to address the people entering the room.

"What's going on here?" A tall security guard asked. He was an older man with a spare tire around his waist and a large beard that covered his neck. "Hey, what happened to those men?"

Parkman moved away from the stretcher to address the guard. He stopped two feet in front of the man.

"Where have you been?" he asked. "There was a fake bomb threat. Two men have been killed on hospital property. Your guys chased the murderer down here and lost her." He turned and pointed at the two doctors dressed in plain clothes on the floor. "Look what she did to those men."

The guard glanced at the morticians, then at Aaron, and back to Parkman.

"I just talked to your superior," Parkman said. "He's up reviewing the cameras." He nodded Aaron's way. "This man is my assistant, Doctor Roberts. We're about to leave with this body to prepare it for the Armstrong Funeral Home." Parkman turned away and went back to the stretcher Sarah rested on. "Now, are we going to have any more delays?"

The guard hesitated, unsure what to do. His radio beeped, and a metallic voice boomed out.

"This is Tankerman," the guard spoke into the radio. "Say again. Over."

Parkman pushed the stretcher. Aaron came around the side to be closer to Tankerman if he became a problem.

The radio crackled in unintelligible English.

They were passing the guard. At the door, Parkman spun the stretcher to the right toward the elevators he'd spied earlier.

"Yes, sir," the guard said from back in the room. "The signal is better. Go ahead. Over."

Aaron ran ahead and pushed the elevator button. The low drone of the lift resonated through the corridor as it descended toward them.

"I see it, sir. But cold storage door number seven is wide open. There's no one inside, sir. The slab is protruding and empty. Maybe I will ask the two doctors I just met down here."

Parkman heard another blast from the radio as the elevator took its sweet time coming down. Aaron waited halfway back down the corridor in case the guard stepped out to pursue them.

"Say again, sir." The guard's loud voice could probably be heard a floor or two above.

The radio crackled at the same moment the elevator doors opened. Parkman silently hoped the lift would be empty and got his wish.

As he pushed the stretcher on, Aaron ran up and joined him.

The guard appeared from the mortician's room, his eyes

wide and his face frantic.

"They're not doctors," the radio was easy to hear now that the guard was out of the room. "Those men are imposters. Stop those men!"

The guard couldn't run with his bulk, but even as he started for the elevator, the doors were closing.

"There's two of them, sir. And they have a body on a stretcher. They're wearing white doctors' clothes, and they're —"

The elevator door cut him off. It began to ascend.

"Whew," Parkman said.

Aaron blew air out between his lips. He seemed to have sobered up in the last few minutes.

Sarah mumbled something. Parkman leaned down.

"You okay?" he asked.

"Hot bath. I need a drink."

"Coming right up."

Aaron moved closer. "We'll go to my apartment. Once there, I'll draw you a bath."

Sarah grunted acknowledgment as the elevator doors opened on the main floor.

Calmly, as if they didn't have a care in the world like they were supposed to be there, Parkman pushed the stretcher while Aaron held the front to steer it. They headed for the back of the hospital as quickly as they could without running.

Cameras followed them at intervals. Near the back doors, Parkman heard people running behind them.

"Grab her, Aaron. Gotta go. Now."

Aaron threw Sarah over his shoulder fireman style and followed Parkman into the rear parking lot.

A yellow taxi was dropping a patient off. The driver was

at the back door on the other side of the car as he helped the elderly woman with her walker.

Aaron dropped Sarah into the back seat. Parkman dropped behind her and rested her head on his lap. When he slammed the door shut, he swung his head back to look at the hospital.

At least a dozen men ran toward them. There was no time to get the driver in the vehicle and get it underway. The cabbie wouldn't leave with that many men shouting for them to stop anyway. Defeated, he looked down at Sarah and almost whispered, *we tried.*

But the car's shocks bounced as Aaron dropped into the driver's seat.

Parkman glanced out the open door where the elderly woman stood at her walker. The cab driver was splayed out on the pavement, just getting to his feet.

Then the taxi shot forward, slamming the back door and cutting off Parkman's view.

In seconds they were on University Avenue and heading deeper into Toronto.

Parkman caressed Sarah's cold forehead and brushed her hair out of her face. He rested his head back and closed his eyes.

Holy shit, that was close.

Chapter 23

THE MORNING SUN BEAT through Aaron's open bedroom curtains.

Heat.

She forgot how much she loved the heat. The cold storage unit hadn't been too bad, but after an hour inside, the temperature had permeated her marrow, chilling her inside and outside. Joints stiffened, and muscles protested the movement. It had been a hassle to continue texting. She'd sent the messages. She could wait. They would come. And they had.

When they'd returned to Aaron's apartment, she'd had the hottest bath of her life with candles and red wine. Then they talked. The three of them talked until after two-thirty in the morning, bringing each other up to speed.

Drained after her long day, she had almost fallen asleep on them on the couch. Aaron carried her to bed and had been a gentleman all night, not touching her other than to cuddle. They needed personal time to discuss things. Their relationship was and had always been founded on respect, understanding, and acceptance. Sex was the glue that kept things together and the oil that kept things moving forward without resistance, but it was never the base. Never, because a sex-based relationship always fell apart. There was a time and a place for sex-based relationships, ones built on lust, but it didn't have a chance with her and Aaron.

She eased his arm off her shoulder and got up to use the toilet. Her limbs were stiff and sore from yesterday. After finishing in the restroom, she walked over to the bedroom's sliding doors and looked outside. A cloudless sky promised a hot and humid day in Toronto.

She jumped at a loud knocking on the apartment door. Aaron was already sitting up in bed when she turned to him.

"Who the fuck is that?" he asked. His eyes turned down to the bedside clock. "And at just after seven in the morning."

The knock came again.

He bolted out of bed, slipped into his jeans, and headed for the front door.

"Stay in here. Hide in the closet if you have to. Don't worry, I'll get rid of whoever it is."

When he got to the living room, Sarah peeked around the corner and saw Parkman, already dressed, waiting for Aaron at the apartment door. Parkman mouthed the words, *a woman.*

Sarah shut the bedroom door quietly and began to get dressed. Aaron kept her spare clothes in his place and hadn't gotten rid of any in her absence. Dressed in faded blue jeans, a tight blue T-shirt, and white socks, Sarah eased to the bedroom door and placed an ear against it.

A female was the only other voice besides Aaron and Parkman. They were discussing Sarah's day and how many people were dead.

She gripped the doorknob and ever so slowly turned it. Once it stopped, she pulled softly, and the bedroom door opened a crack. The voices doubled in volume without the door as a barrier.

She listened for half a minute, then opened the door all the way. From her vantage point, no one was visible, which meant they were all sitting in the living room.

"We have to find Sarah," the woman said. "This needs to end. The city is in a panic."

"Now c'mon, the city isn't in a panic," Parkman said. "That girl was going to jump. You said so yourself. And that couple who were killed near Orillia were found with multiple victims inside their house. Whoever shot that couple—"

"Sarah Roberts shot Joel and Belinda," the woman interjected.

"Allegedly," Parkman said, ignoring her interruption. "Whoever shot those people did the public a favor."

"But that's not how it works, and you, of all people, should know that, Parkman. I know the friends you have on the force. And I know how well-liked Sarah is, but this has to end. She needs to come in and answer for what she has done. There's no other way out of this mess."

"And you came here today thinking she'd be here?" Aaron asked.

"Where else? You were both witnessed at the hospital last night. My partner was there. When he texted me the pictures from the hospital cameras, I knew where to go next." She cleared her throat. "Out of respect to you and the Sarah we all know, I came alone. But I can't guarantee who else will be coming." She coughed and cleared her throat again. "So, where is she?"

Vivian whispered to Sarah. In seconds, Sarah understood that this woman, Detective Marina Diner, was an asset and would help complete her tasks in Toronto. Sarah understood everything as she stepped into the room and stood behind Aaron's armchair.

Marina gasped and stopped pacing by the glass doors that led to the balcony. Parkman widened his eyes and raised his eyebrows. He already had a toothpick in his mouth.

Same old Parkman.

Sarah leaned down and whispered in Aaron's ear. He nodded. She moved to the side of Aaron's chair while he stood.

Marina was a pretty woman in her forties. She had a strong figure for her age, lean and tight like a part-time runner and bodybuilder. She had to spend considerable time in the gym for a physique like that. In her black dress pants, white collared shirt, and light suit jacket, she looked like the stereotypical detective, the kind found on movie posters. Any woman who cared for herself this well in a man's world deserved respect.

"Well, I must say, I'm surprised to see you." Diner's eyes dropped to Sarah's sock feet and rose until they met Sarah's eyes. "You're a lot smaller in person than I expected."

"I've gotten that before."

"Did you step out of the back room to resist arrest? Or are you turning yourself in?"

"Neither."

Diner started across the living room floor tentatively, one foot in front of the other, then a pause, then one more step.

"You don't have a lot of options, young lady. You're going to have to come with me."

"I came out of the bedroom to talk."

"Fine." Diner stopped in front of her and pulled the cuffs off her belt. "We can talk, but come on, Sarah. This can't go on. I have to take you in. If it isn't me, then who knows what police officer will arrest you and how trigger-happy they will be after you murdered Simmons last night."

Sarah forgot how fast Aaron was. After achieving a black belt in Shotokan Karate many years ago, he opened a dojo and taught others until they reached the black belt level. He had three amazing teachers working at his dojo who once saved his life in Greece. He owed them everything, including the success of his business.

When he was focused, honed as he was now, he was silent, fast, and efficient, every muscle having the exact amount of use, tension, and thrust during a subdued handhold and lockdown. In under a second, Diner was forced back away from Sarah, manhandled to her knees, and absolutely immobilized. Aaron locked her hands behind her head, her legs bent back under the weight of her own fallen body. Her neck was cocked at an angle that even mild struggle appeared to cause pain.

"I'd suggest you be still," Sarah said, her voice soft and feminine. It was hard to be the alpha she portrayed in the street when Aaron was in the room. He was too much alpha for all four of them put together. Even Parkman had leaned back on the couch and crossed his legs like he was about to have an afternoon cup of tea. "I'm going to remove your weapon and car keys now." Sarah pulled Diner's gun and slipped it into the back of her pants. The car keys she dropped in her pocket. Then she nodded at Aaron.

Almost faster than the eye, he released the grip on her hands, pulled her arms down and around her back, and cuffed her. Professional that she was, not a single peep of protest was issued from her.

He released the detective, crab-walked backward away from her, and got to his feet, barely an extra breath of effort for his trouble.

Fuck, I love this guy. Jerk that he is sometimes, that was special to watch.

As Diner struggled to her feet, Sarah stared at Aaron.

"You have to teach me that shit," she said. "That was good."

Aaron offered a barely perceptible nod as Parkman got off the couch and helped Diner to a sitting position. Clearly, she hadn't been in cuffs too often. Then, on a count of three, he lifted her onto the couch. Her pelvis stuck out as she made room for her bound hands behind her.

"And what will this solve?" Diner asked, a wisp of hair dangling in her right eye. She stuck out her lower lip and puffed it away.

Sarah sat in Aaron's chair, facing Diner. Parkman was back in his spot on the sofa, as casual as ever, toothpick wandering back and forth across his lips. Aaron pulled a chair from the dining room table and sat.

"Everything can be explained," Sarah said. "For the right person to listen."

"I'm not that person," Diner responded. "A judge is. A

jury. It's only my job to bring the suspects in and build a case."

"I disagree." Sarah leaned back and brought her knees up, resting her feet on the chair. "Aaron, can we have some coffee while we talk?"

"Gladly." He got up and disappeared into the kitchen.

"I didn't kill Detective Simmons last night."

"Then who did? My partner was an eyewitness."

"They have Samantha Mason, your partner's wife," Sarah said, her voice soft. This was going to be a calm conversation. She needed Diner on her side, or Diner wouldn't leave the apartment until everything was finished in Toronto.

"Who has Samantha?" Diner asked.

"Your partner Niles fucked up, and they're making him pay for it."

Diner's attention was locked on Sarah.

"Fucked up?" she asked. "How?"

"He saw Vanessa Simmons with them and let her out the warehouse's back door. They lifted his fingerprints off the door knob. Beyond that, I have no idea where this warehouse is or who is involved, but I'll know soon."

"What?" Diner looked completely perplexed.

The kettle in the kitchen had reached a high pitch. Then the grinder started as Aaron ground the coffee beans for the French press. Sarah waited so she didn't have to compete with the noise from the kitchen. The grinder stopped, the kettle beeped, and the noise diminished.

"I'm not entirely sure yet," Sarah said.

"About what?" Diner adjusted herself on the sofa. "Am I getting any of that coffee?"

Sarah shook her head. "You're not coming out of those cuffs until I'm satisfied you're on our side."

An exasperated puff of air blew out of Diner's mouth. "I figure preaching to you about all the laws you're breaking right now wouldn't matter."

Sarah shook her head. "It would only matter if I cared. The bad guys never worry about your laws. The only way to catch or stop them is to not play by the rules. Now, to get coffee, you have to be on our side. Interested?"

"I'll never be on your side. I'm a cop, not a vigilante."

Sarah shrugged. "Then you don't drink coffee."

Aaron entered the room with three cups. He placed one beside Sarah, one by Parkman, and then sat by the dining room table with his.

"I'll start at the beginning to offer you an understanding. If you're not going to help us, you surely won't be stopping us." She sipped from her cup. "Your partner, Mason, helped Simmons's daughter Vanessa escape from a warehouse. She had ventured there on her own by accident. I'm not entirely sure how she got there, but it had to do with looking for her father. After a few days, she got stuck there. At first, they tried to convince her to partake in warehouse activities. Upon her refusal, they drugged her food. In her stupor, she was raped repeatedly."

Sarah paused to sip from her mug. "When they discovered—"

"Who's they?" Diner snapped.

"This only comes out once, as I have to leave soon. I'm offering everything I know. I won't leave anything out. If I knew who they were, I would tell you." Sarah tightened her jaw. "No more interruptions. Or Aaron will hogtie, gag, and place you in the back closet for a week. Do not push me. I never bluff."

Diner glanced at Aaron, who set his coffee down and glared at her. Parkman shrugged.

Then Aaron said, "This is Sarah's show. I just do what she says. Best you do, too."

Sarah didn't wait for Diner to look back at her before she started talking again.

"They kidnapped Mason's wife Samantha the next night and offered Mason a way back in to make things right after letting Vanessa escape." She drank from her cup, feeling the warmth ooze down her throat and into her stomach. It calmed her further after last night's morgue visit. "His task was to kill Detective Simmons. I was getting close, though, so they ordered him to execute me, too. He was told his wife would be freed, unharmed."

Diner was shaking her head.

"But," Sarah added. "Mason's wife Samantha is already being ... used. I'm sorry."

"How are your fingerprints on the murder weapon that killed Detective Simmons?" Diner asked. "They came back positive this morning."

"Simmons was about to murder me in the parking lot when Mason killed him. Then Mason tossed the gun at me. In the dark, I couldn't see what he tossed until it was in my hands."

Diner looked away from Sarah. She was angry. It showed in her eyes, the tight-set jaw, and the clenching facial muscles. Diner didn't believe her but wasn't ready to call her a liar.

"Mason didn't go with you to Orillia yesterday," Sarah

said. "He needed to stay behind and deal with Simmons and me. At the CN Tower, we both know that Vanessa was about to fall and there was no saving her, but a suicide only gets buried. A murder victim gets a lot more attention. Killing Joel and Belinda is explained away. You'd shoot them too if you found what I found in that house."

"There's more," Diner mumbled.

"More? What do you mean, more?"

"We found a makeshift grave. At least a dozen other bodies are buried behind that house in Orillia. They're still up there digging. It's turning into Ontario's version of the Pickton murders."

"Pickton murders?" Sarah asked, glancing at Parkman. "Not sure I've heard of that one."

"In British Columbia," Parkman cut in, "Robert Pickton was convicted in 2007 for the murder of six women and charged in the death of over twenty more, but those charges were stayed."

"Wow, you keep up on Canadian affairs, Parkman. Impressed."

"That was a big one. I read the online papers."

"I have enough criminals in my life on a day-to-day basis," Sarah said. "I don't read about them online. But I have heard of Paul Bernardo here in Ontario since the early nineties."

"Yeah," Diner was shaking her head again. "That was before I made detective. But discussing serial killers and murderers won't get us anywhere. We could spend all afternoon talking about Jeffrey Dahmer, Karl Toft, Ed Gein, Ted Bundy, and Charlie Manson, but we'll be no closer to what you're doing." She paused and tilted her head back in thought, staring at the stucco ceiling. "Or are you trying to outdo them, Sarah, thinking you're justified in some way?"

"Let me ask you a question," Sarah said, leaning forward and placing her elbows on the armrests, coffee cup cradled in both hands. Sarah's coffee was half gone. She took a large pull from it and set the cup on the table by her chair.

"If you knew what Hitler was capable of before the war, say in 1936 or 1937, and you had a chance to take him out, would you?"

"No."

"You have an answer that fast? So you've thought of that question before?"

"Yes."

"Why?" Sarah asked.

"Because a lot of senseless lives were taken during the war, families destroyed, and I'm sorry for that, but in the end, this world has changed because of him. The Geneva Convention. The new laws. The world stops people like Saddam Hussein now. Who knows what the world would look like if Hitler hadn't risen to power?"

"You're crazy," Sarah said. "Sorry, but that's ridiculous, in my opinion. Too many families and people suffered because of one man's lunacy. Granted, I wasn't there, but if I knew what I know now, I wouldn't just kill him, I'd tear his intestines out and put all thirty feet of them on display for the world to see."

"And you'd be imprisoned or killed for it," Diner responded, her voice sharp and curt.

"You're right. And you want to know why? Because fate is what it is? Bit of a lame argument, don't ya think?"

"Whatever." Diner adjusted herself on the sofa. With her

hands cuffed behind her, she appeared to be getting more uncomfortable as they talked. "Say what you have to say to me. You're running out of time. There will be a dozen police officers busting that door down within the hour."

"Bullshit." Sarah let her feet fall to the floor and stretched her legs. "You checked Aaron's history and read his file. You looked up Parkman. You didn't believe they would harbor a fugitive. You figured they wouldn't tell you where I was, but you knew I wouldn't be here, or you wouldn't have come alone. At least that's what you counted on. But you did come alone because Detective Mason is attending to other business. He's checking with his colleagues to see if his wife can come home now. But therein lies the problem for him. Samantha Mason is in the basement of a Chinese restaurant being worked over by a small contingent of a Chinese gang."

"And how do you know all this?"

"You obviously don't know me very well."

Diner leaned forward on the sofa. "What was that with all the Hitler talk?"

"I wanted you to better understand why I killed Fletcher Aldrich's father. He was the mastermind of the consortium in Toronto that I'm here to break up. He started it, and his sons took over. When there was a dispute about Joel's behavior, he was banned but continued his evil ways on his own property in Orillia. Fletcher's father was evil incarnate, a despicable man who should have been killed fifty years ago. Hundreds of women have been murdered because of him."

"Preposterous. Absolutely ridiculous." Diner was working herself up. She tugged on her cuffs and tried to get comfortable on the couch. "We would have caught on to someone like that years ago. We're not some half-baked detective crew eating donuts all the time. And what consortium are you talking about?"

Sarah rose from her chair. "I'll need your car and your gun to free Samantha Mason. So thanks for the loan."

"What about me? With murder charges pending, I understand that kidnapping a detective isn't much, but I'm still wondering, what about me?"

"When I'm in position, or when Samantha is with me, these men here will take you somewhere unharmed and take the cuffs off. Until this is completely over, Parkman and Aaron will not return to this apartment."

"You'll all be hunted down like the fugitives you are," Diner blurted out.

"Fate, right?" Sarah nodded. "We'll take our chances. When you discover the whole truth, you'll understand what motivated me. You might see things differently."

"I'm sure I won't. Right is right. Wrong is wrong. Murder is never the way. Never."

"Really? Okay, I'll remember that." Sarah pulled Detective Simmons's cell phone out. "After Simmons was killed in front of me yesterday, his cell phone dropped virtually in my lap. I grabbed it. Here, read this text."

Sarah held it in front of the detective.

"That's the name of a missing persons case that's a month old," Diner said. "What's the address for?"

"Here's another from the month before."

Sarah showed Diner, then pulled the phone away.

"Don't know that name," Diner said.

Sarah flipped a few buttons on the phone and held it for Diner to look at once more.

"That name I know," the detective said. "Another

missing person. Why are they on Simmons's phone?"

"These are the names of nomads, wanderers who came to Toronto for fast cash, hooking on the side. No family, no friends. He sent one name per month and probably received payment for it."

"These girls," Diner paused. She bit her lower lip, released it, and said, "These girls are gone now?"

"They were picked up. The warehouse has them. The same place Vanessa escaped."

"If Mason helped her escape this warehouse you're talking about, what was *he* doing there?"

"You'll have to ask him yourself. Something tells me you'll see him later today. Oh, one last thing."

Sarah flipped through Simmons's received calls list until she stopped on a number. Then she showed it to Diner.

"Know this number?"

Diner shook her head. "Should I?"

"Parkman looked the number up. It belongs to Councilman Marshall Machiavelli. Name mean anything to you?"

"I know who he is if that's what you mean. Maybe Simmons and Machiavelli were friends."

"Maybe." Sarah got up and walked around her chair. "Maybe. Something tells me we'll find everything out very soon."

She walked away. In the bedroom, she grabbed a pad and a pen and made a note for Aaron. After ripping the paper off, she headed back to the living room.

She put her shoes on at the door and gestured for Aaron to come over.

"This ends today. Here." she held out the note. "Take

this. Read it and do what it says. These are Vivian's words." She kissed him long and hard, biting his lower lip softly. She pulled away and said, "Let Detective Diner go to her office. There she will find a search warrant. Assure her she'll want to execute it. Then meet me at the warehouse address on this note. I'll need a ride to the airport."

"Why? Where are you going? And what's at this warehouse?"

"I have no idea what I'm in for. All I know is what Vivian had me write down. Just don't fuck any of this up."

"Anything for me to do?" Parkman asked.

"Yeah, the same as Aaron. Follow what the note says to a tee."

"What about me?" Diner asked.

"I'll be seeing you later. Aaron will explain. You will have all the evidence you need for your court system."

Sarah turned to leave.

"Where are you going?" Diner asked.

"To catch me some bad guys." She stuck her head out the apartment door, then turned and looked back. "Oh, and thanks for the use of the car."

"You're using it against my will," Diner shouted. "And don't get a scratch on it!"

"You mean I'm stealing it?" Sarah asked in a high-pitched little girl voice.

"Yes, you're stealing it."

"Oooh, cool."

Aaron stepped in close. "Stay safe, woman," he whispered in her ear.

"I always do. Thanks for having my back."

Sarah stepped away, hopped on one foot, and ran down

the hallway.

She didn't want to be late because Samantha's life had little time left. As far as Vivian would reveal, it might already be too late.

Chapter 24

Outside the apartment building, Sarah pushed Detective Diner's key fob seven times before a car horn beeped to let her know where Diner had parked. Upstairs, it hadn't crossed her mind to ask.

She headed toward the horn's short, sharp noise but stopped a few cars away.

This can't be right.

An old green car with shiny rims was parked in a visitor's parking spot. Sarah pushed the fob once more. The green car's horn beeped.

"Wow, Detective, I would have never pictured you for the muscle car type."

Sarah circled the vehicle. It was a Pontiac Catalina, circa the late sixties, maybe early seventies. She opened the driver's door to a pristine interior, everything polished and spotless. It looked so clean, Diner must have it detailed weekly. She ran her hand along the car's body and felt the power, the steel, and knew how heavy this older model vehicle was.

At least heading for that Chinese restaurant would be fun in this thing.

Sarah got in, started the engine, felt its low rumble, and then peeled out of the lot. She turned on the stereo system and played the CD in the dash. Skrillex shot out of the speakers.

"Interesting taste, Detective."

After heading south a few city blocks, then across Queen Street and up Spadina toward China Town, Sarah located the restaurant by psychic magnetism as Vivian guided her. When she looked at the front of the building, she knew it for what it was. Not a restaurant but a drop location. A place that took payments facilitated the movement of cocaine locally and was a big import-export player. Shipments were narcotics, but also humans. The food serving part of the restaurant was only there so deals could be made over chicken chow mein and sweet and sour chicken balls.

The street was lined with vehicles. She eased by the restaurant slowly and watched the building. The two men acting nonchalant and chatting on cell phones out front were security. The one on the right had a shoulder holster exposed. She had to assume the building was wired with cameras, and like a casino, those cameras were always monitored by someone in a back room.

Maybe she would try the rear door or a window at the side of the building. There had to be a way in without walking through the front door.

Garbage littered the sidewalk, and the smell of the area

came off the already-hot pavement. The sidewalks were scattered with hundreds of people shopping, touring, and preparing for lunch. Ill-equipped with a small gun, she had no idea how to get inside and rescue Samantha Mason.

Sarah turned up a side street half a block away and parked by a garbage bin. She kept the car away from the brick wall of the building to her right so she could use the passenger door if she needed it to get Samantha inside fast.

After turning off the Pontiac, Sarah checked her mirrors and removed her seatbelt.

"I'm here, sis," she said to the empty car. "What now?"

At first, nothing came, even though Sarah could feel Vivian was close.

"Vivian? Anything? Any ideas on how you want me to get inside this restaurant and extract—"

Get down!

Sarah reacted instantly, lying across the seat of the Catalina. It was like a sofa, one long piece.

"What was that for?" Sarah whispered. Her hand snaked back and withdrew Diner's gun, her eyes on the driver's side window. "You gonna tell me why you yelled in my head like that? It's disorientating. Scares the fuck out of me."

Chinese voices bickered about something close by. Cautiously, Sarah sat up high enough to use the passenger side mirror to look behind the car, then ducked back down.

"Holy shit, holy shit," she muttered over and over.

She fumbled for her cell phone, hit 911, and got directed to the police department. As the line clicked, the Chinese voices outside stopped arguing.

"Police, what's the emergency?"

Sarah checked the mirror once more. Earlier, there had

been three, but now five men fanned out behind the Pontiac Catalina. Each man carried a large machine gun slung over his shoulder. But now, all five men had them aimed at the Pontiac.

"What's the emergency?" the 911 dispatcher asked again. "Is someone there? Are you all right?"

Sarah opened her mouth to speak but was cut off as a cacophony of machine guns erupted behind the car. The cell phone dropped out of her hand and fell to the floor mats as she moved to cover her head. The vehicle shook violently from the assault of the fusillade. The back window burst inward, covering her in bits of tempered glass. She couldn't hear herself scream as the bullets rained down.

For fear of the car's gas tank exploding, she wanted to get out, but the thought of moving anywhere, let alone into the open without the protection of the car, kept her immobile.

Then, just as fast as it started, it stopped. She panted like she'd just come up from underwater after being submerged too long. She moved to check the mirrors, but both outside mirrors were shattered. Glass covered the seat and floor. Even the front windshield was broken in multiple places.

Diner's going to kill me.

Without eyes on her surroundings, her attackers could be walking up to the car on either side, and she wouldn't know about it. She had to get out of the car.

Using the tip of her shoe, she pulled the door handle toward her and pushed outward with her other foot. The driver's side door popped open. The second it was open all the way, gunfire exploded from behind, shattering the inside panel. Chunks of plastic, liner, and little bits of metal danced from the assault and came to rest on the pavement below.

She let out a small scream and reached for the passenger side door, shoving it open. Then she thrust forward and was about to climb out the passenger side head first when more bullets hit that side. The door was destroyed to the point where it broke free from the car's body and dangled at a forty-five-degree angle.

The guns wouldn't let up. There was no way out. A deadly hail of bullets cut off all routes of escape. She screamed at the injustice. Why allow her to park here? Why did Vivian let it end like this?

Through the front windshield, from her spread-out position on the front seat, Sarah stared up at the blue sky, panting, mouth open, covered in a cool sweat. She had been through a lot but had never been held down like this by machine guns. Diner's small weapon would be no match for the five men behind her vehicle.

At any moment, one of those men would walk up beside the car, spin their hand cannon toward Sarah, and empty their magazine until her body succumbed in an epileptic death dance.

The distant whoop of a police siren felt like safety, security. But there was no way those men would walk away, the job incomplete. This wasn't a warning. This was a death squad, and they had left her with no play.

Glass crunched underfoot nearby.

The police were still too far away. Her life would be over in seconds.

Vivian wouldn't leave her in this situation without a way out.

Glass crunched again. Sarah assessed how close they were. Then closed her eyes and whispered to Vivian to help in locating them.

She counted to one.

Slipped her finger inside the trigger guard.

Counted to two.

Applied pressure on the trigger.

Three.

She opened her eyes, sat up, aimed out the broken back window, and shot the man standing by the trunk three times in the chest. Even as he fell, red bursting up on his chest where Sarah's bullets entered, the four remaining men twenty feet back opened fire on the Pontiac again. This time they didn't stop until they emptied their weapons and had to reload.

Sarah screamed along with the assault, waiting for their ammunition to pierce the back of the car at the right angle, enter through the back seat and continue through the front seat and into her. With her head between her arms and legs scrunched up, covered in glass and various other pieces of upholstery, an idea occurred to her.

She couldn't exit the car through the doors, and going out the broken back window would be stepping into the line of fire.

But the broken front windshield was another case entirely.

Quickly, before they could reload and continue toward the car, Sarah swung her legs around and kicked at the windshield with both feet. Two hard stomps later and it disconnected from the frame in almost one piece. It landed on the hood, slid down, and fell off slightly to the right.

She pivoted on the seat, got her feet under her, and twisted around to fire her weapon out the back window.

The four men were just bringing their weapons around to aim at the destroyed Pontiac Catalina as Sarah's bullets went wide. It had the effect she wanted as each man ducked aside and spread out to avoid being hit.

She pushed off with her feet and dove through the open windshield, holding the gun tight. Her shoulder took the hit on the hood of the car before she rolled off and smacked onto the pavement. Before she could catch her breath, she looked under the car for anyone approaching, but the alleyway behind the Pontiac was empty now.

The four Chinese assassins had disappeared. Only the body of the one she shot was visible.

Police sirens were pulling up out front of the restaurant and at the mouth of the road she had parked on. It had been a long time since she was happy to have the police arrive.

Weakened by the ordeal, her muscles jelly-like, she pushed off the dirty ground, slipped Diner's gun away, and got to her feet. A minor tremble went through her knees. She leaned on the hood of the car and examined the extensive damage.

How the hell did I survive that?

Men ran into the street and looked her way.

"Hey," one shouted. "You there. Freeze!"

Sarah turned away and hobbled into a back alley. Finding strength from somewhere, she ran to the end of the alley until she realized she was standing behind the Chinese restaurant that held Samantha Mason.

The back door was opening. She caught a glimpse of a uniform as she slipped behind two large garbage dumpsters. Stained cardboard boxes and wooden crates were piled high by one dumpster. She edged behind them and covered her feet with a crate. The smell of rotting food was overwhelming. Scents of rot and decay came off black gunk piled under her shoulder blades. Grease or used vegetable oil piled an inch thick already oozed through her T-shirt. A mouse scurried inside the crate beside her head, dining on a half-eaten piece of something that might have once been lemon chicken.

She retched silently as the smell was so horrid she could taste the rot. She covered her mouth fast enough to quell any noise as men drew near her position.

A few words came her way. They were talking about a woman. Something about a funeral home. The two officers who had chased her from the Pontiac stepped close to the garbage bins.

The mouse turned to watch her. Its tiny nose sniffed the air, its whiskers jerking back and forth. Then it moved closer and sniffed the air again.

If she screamed now, it was over. There could be no coming back from this. No resolution to her Toronto tasks, and the people she hunted would get away with everything.

Come on, Sarah. Get tougher. Like the old days. Fuck this situation and everything about it. You're better than a shit mouse.

She tightened her jaw, clenched her fists, and then paid attention to the men on the other side of the garbage bins.

One of the lids opened and slammed down.

"Hey, what are you doing there?" someone asked.

For a brief second, Sarah thought they had discovered her and that the voice was addressed to her.

"We followed the girl down here, Councilor. Just checking to see if she jumped in one of these bins to hide."

Councilor?

The other bin's lid slammed back into place.

"Carry on. No one ran down this way."

"Yes, sir."

The man they called Councilor moved closer. She couldn't see him from her position, but another man walked with him.

"We almost got her. Had her pinned down in that car. What happened?"

"The police got here," another voice said. "Someone else must've called them."

"Okay, find her. Kill her. We can dispose of the body at the funeral home."

Funeral home? The same one Vivian asked Aaron to meet me at in the note she left him? Sarah closed her eyes. *Golly, thanks, Vivian. Guess I'm dead, is that it?*

"What about the woman's body?"

"Take Samantha's corpse to the funeral home, too. I'm meeting Niles Mason there later. They can cremate together. Then we cremate the stupid girl, and it's done. This whole mess will end. Now, leave me. I have to make a call."

One set of steps moved out of earshot. A moment later, the councilor started talking, but he had turned away from her and whispered something unintelligible.

She was too late.

Samantha Mason had been killed. This councilor was responsible, and now he was going to kill Detective Niles Mason.

She eased Diner's empty gun out and quietly escaped her hiding place behind the garbage bins.

It was time to turn the heat up.

It was time to stop the murders by killing a few more assholes.

214

Chapter 25

After easing out from under the crates, Sarah crouched behind the dumpster and scanned the alleyway. The councilor talked on his phone five feet away, near the back of a Lincoln Continental.

Marshall Machiavelli.

"That's what I'm saying," Machiavelli said into his phone, his back to Sarah as she stood to her full height. "The fact that that meddling bitch was in the vicinity makes the plan work. Explain during your press conference that Sarah Roberts has murdered again and Samantha Mason, a cop's wife, was the victim. That's why there's a large police presence here now. Say that we're locking the area down to find Samantha's murderer, an American named Sarah Roberts. The public will believe it."

Anger rose in her as she moved closer to him, focusing on the back of the councilor's head.

The rear door of the restaurant banged open as a cop jumped out. Machiavelli turned at the noise, but Sarah sprang into action.

She wrapped her free arm around the councilor's neck, yanked him back into her, and brought Diner's gun up to his cheek.

"Drop it!" the cop at the restaurant shouted. He moved closer, lowering a few steps as more officers exited the restaurant behind him. "I'll take the shot. Drop the fucking gun."

Machiavelli's hands moved skyward, the cell phone still locked in his grip, as Sarah spun him around to protect herself from itchy triggers.

"Tell them to back off," she ordered Machiavelli. "If I take a bullet, you do too." She jammed the tip of the gun into his cheek hard enough to bruise his gums. He grunted and tilted his head to the side to ease the pressure.

"Okay, okay."

Seven uniformed officers had now emerged from the restaurant's back door, guns up and ready. At any moment, one of them would try to play the hero. This wasn't working. The door opened again as more tried to come out.

"Tell them to remain calm," Sarah whispered. "I don't have to remind you what I did to Vanessa, Joel, Belinda, and Fletcher's dad."

"Okay, everyone take it easy," Machiavelli shouted.

"We're going for a ride in your car," Sarah said. "Mine needs some work now."

"We're leaving," the councilor shouted for the cops to hear.

"Can't let you do that, sir," the officer who had come out

first said. "Have to apprehend her."

"You're not listening, Officer. She will kill me like she has killed so many in the past two days." Sarah started backing him up toward the Continental. "I'll be fine," Machiavelli went on. "Just don't play hero and get me shot."

"They can lower their weapons, too," Sarah chimed in.

"Lower them," Machiavelli ordered.

Sarah and Machiavelli stood against the side of his car. None of the officer's guns lowered.

Sarah's temper flared. She drew back on her arm, choking Machiavelli, and forced him to arch backward and raise onto the tips of his shoes, the whole time keeping Diner's gun jammed into the side of his face.

"Lower them means," she whispered, then shouted, "lower the *fucking* guns."

Machiavelli was making choking sounds, his hands scrabbling at Sarah's arm. Remarkably, his cell phone never left his grip. Sarah eased the pressure off, lowering him to the soles of his feet. He choked, gasped, and then coughed to clear a path in his throat to breathe.

"Open the door," Sarah said.

Machiavelli reached around and pulled the back door to his Lincoln open.

"I'm going in backward. You follow. Stupid shit gets you dead. Understood?"

He nodded, not ready to speak yet.

Sarah made him bend his knees as she got in the car. Vivian whispered to her that the car had a driver and that the driver was unarmed and willing to drive.

Then the upholstery of the Continental's back seat met her butt. She eased back carefully and pulled Machiavelli down with her.

He got inside the vehicle without a problem. Sarah moved the gun until it was placed at the opening of his ear, then reached over him to slam the door shut.

"Go!" she yelled at the driver.

The car got underway immediately. She chanced a look out the back window and saw about a dozen cops running after the car, half of them talking into little radios attached to their epaulets. Then she sunk lower in the seat to reduce her head being a target.

"No need to worry," Machiavelli said. "This car is bulletproof."

Sarah sat back up, feeling a little foolish. They wouldn't open fire on her in the councilor's car as long as he was with her. Nerves after what happened to the Pontiac Catalina had made her duck.

She slid along the seat to the other side of the car and rested the gun on her lap, keeping it aimed in his direction.

"Thank you," he said.

"For what?"

"Moving away."

She frowned.

"You stink. What's that smell?"

"Oh, that. It's a new collection of perfumes from Toronto's finest importers and exporters of human beings. It's called Garbage Scent. It also comes in Human Waste scent and, for those special assholes, Scum of the Earth scent. I got too close to you, hence the smell." She offered him a wry, half smile, then pursed her lips. "Tell me how you thought you could get away unscathed?"

The driver turned up another road, then ran a yellow and

headed south on Spadina.

"How about you?" he asked, turning to face her. "With all the murders you've committed, do you really think there's anywhere in this world you can go to escape prosecution?"

"Maybe I'll kill every criminal in Toronto. That'll help me escape justice."

Machiavelli tried to stifle a laugh, but his mouth closed too late.

"That makes no sense whatsoever," he said.

"I once heard someone say, kill a few people, and you're called a murderer. Kill a few million, and you're a conqueror."

"Is that what you're trying to do here? Conquer Toronto?"

Sarah shook her head. "No, not really. I'm only here to stop you."

She looked out the window. The car was heading under the raised Gardener Expressway at the base of Spadina. In a block or so, the driver would have to turn left or right, or they'd end up in Lake Ontario.

When she turned back to Machiavelli, he had a wide grin on his face.

"What could you possibly find so amusing?" Sarah asked.

"Your face."

"Bold statement for a man in your position, seeing as I'm the one with the weapon."

The car stopped in the middle of an intersection. He had to be waiting to turn left. She needed more time to decide where to send him. The warehouse or the funeral home? But where were those buildings?

Where should I go, Vivian?

"You may have the weapon," Machiavelli said. "But not for very long."

"How's that? You're going to disarm me?" She braced herself for him if, in fact, that was what he wanted to do.

"No. They are." He pointed behind her.

"So old, so old. That trick." She wagged a finger at him.

The car still hadn't moved. Through the windshield, no vehicles approached them. The driver wasn't waiting to turn left after all.

Sarah dove across the seat and landed on Machiavelli just as something made of at least a dozen tons of steel smacked into the Lincoln. The car was shoved sideways until the wheels met the curb. It lifted at a forty-five-degree angle and hovered a moment, Sarah twisted uncomfortably, her face plastered against the passenger side window, then descended back to the road, smacking hard, the chassis protesting the hit.

Before she could regain her balance and locate Diner's gun that had been knocked from her grip, something else smacked the car from behind. It was shoved forward, and Sarah was pushed into the back of the seat, her shoulder twisting at an odd angle, pain shooting through her upper neck.

Another hit, but this time she saw what was attacking them. Three large pickup trucks with huge thick bars covering their grills were taking turns playing smashup derby with the Continental, which was losing poorly.

Another hit knocked her to the floor of the back seat. As she struggled to get up, one of the trucks hit them again, this time crunching in the side door enough that Sarah got wedged in and stuck.

"Shit!" she yelled as a deeper pain coursed through her shoulder. "Nothing had better be broken."

Machiavelli's door ripped open. Two men hauled him out and helped him away. Then a man carrying a long-barreled weapon came into sight.

"Get out," he said.

"Nope. Can't move. Stuck."

Someone yanked on the door that held her in place. After two loud metallic bangs, the bent door gave way and popped open, exposing Sarah.

Rough hands wrapped around her shoulders and yanked upward as she screamed at the pain.

This isn't working out too well, sis.

The hands pulled her free, then dropped her. After one bounce on the concrete with her head, stars formed in her vision.

She looked under the Lincoln, then spun her head frantically to look the other way, wincing at the pain in her shoulder. The sunlight was cut off by someone standing over her.

Machiavelli moved in close. He held a baseball bat, the trunk of the Continental open behind him.

"You'll burn for this, bitch."

The tip of the bat came in hard and too fast to avoid. It connected with her head and turned the lights out.

Chapter 26

Someone screamed. A man in pain. A lot of pain. All of it from underwater. Distant somehow.

Consciousness swam up violently. Faint light filled her vision. A spotlight, but not on her, shone on the center of the tiled floor. Like a hospital floor. Her cheek ached. Her shoulder throbbed. Random thoughts flitted through her head.

Chinese restaurant. Vegetable oil. Grease. Smell. The car. The accident.

The baseball bat.

She opened her eyes and gasped. She was on the floor in a room similar to the morgue in a hospital's basement.

A man stood beside her. She turned her head slowly. Another man stood on the other side of her.

She adjusted her weight, moved slightly to the right, and sat up, testing her shoulder as she rose until her back leaned on a bank of cupboards. A cool dribble of saliva had pooled at the corner of her mouth. It leaked down her chin. When she wiped it, she felt the swelling the baseball bat had caused. A close inspection with her tongue revealed all her teeth were in the right places.

She smiled, frowned, and opened her mouth wide, then closed it. No broken cheekbones. Only an ache in the face that felt like a sadomasochistic brick had kissed her too hard.

The scream again. Coming from the other room.

She looked up at the men beside her. Both wore suits. Were they the mafia, the FBI, or well-dressed businessmen? Weapons were strapped over their shoulders. Large guns that could easily release multiple bullets in rapid succession.

A shadow filled the door. A man entered and turned on the main light.

"Ahh, she's awake." Councilor Marshall Machiavelli moved inside the room and stopped at a metal table. "How was your sleep?"

"Could have used a cocktail first. Maybe a whiskey." The slight discomfort in her cheek made her wince and case the words out with limited use of her mouth, but her shoulder was already feeling better. Probably just a sore muscle; nothing pulled.

"I, unfortunately, didn't have any alcohol readily available when our little accident happened. But none of that will matter soon enough."

"How and when does whiskey never matter?" she asked.

"Touché. You're so right. I think I'll enjoy a double when this is all over. One for you and one for me."

He maneuvered the metal table—an oversized gurney—until it was aimed at her.

"Let me ask you something," Machiavelli said.

Sarah looked at the door Machiavelli had just come through. Someone else was in the room beyond that door. How many men were present? If she could disarm one of the guards standing on either side of her, maybe the weapon they carried could help her leave this place.

"You're so masculine and strong," Machiavelli said. "You have to tell me."

She turned to glare at him.

"You must have a set of balls dangling from each side of your labia. That testosterone bath babies get must have come with something extra for you, right? Or do you still have testosterone baths regularly? Am I correct here? Because no woman could ever destroy so much in such a short time unless you were from some Mexican cartel or elite mafia hit squad." He glanced at the men on either side of her. "Maybe she's with the Mossad or MI6. Could be we have a hero among us." Machiavelli met her gaze, a wide smile creasing his features. "A *super*hero. Wow." He placed his hands on his hips in mock surprise. "Isn't that something? A real, true-life superhero in our presence. Well," he walked around the table and grabbed thick gloves off the counter, "we can't have superheroes going around killing the citizens of Toronto, now can we?"

"I agree," Sarah said. "So how about I just kill you? Then I'll have that double whiskey, and I'll leave Toronto. When I get home, I'll shave my ball sac and think about getting them removed as you'll be dead, and I won't need them anymore. Sound good?"

"Being pretty gets you a few points." He stopped in front of her and bent over, placing his gloved hands on his knees.

"Being smoking hot gets you extra points. Man, the things I could do to you. I'd tear your pussy in half and come inside you so much you'd taste it a month later while you're throwing up."

Sarah fought the urge to spit in his face.

"But being a man-chick, that costs you points. Being sarcastic has put you in the negative. Now you're not pretty anymore, and you definitely won't be hot in about fifteen minutes. Well, actually, you'll be hot, just not in the sense you think I mean. The fires of a cremation make you really hot. The searing kind."

"Fire? Cremation? Really?"

"You'll bathe in the flames of cremation soon enough. But first." He stood back up and nodded at the men.

They grabbed her under the arms, spun her around, and laid her on her back, her feet planted against the cupboards she had been leaning against moments ago.

When they let go, and before she could struggle back around, both men lowered their weapons and lightly touched her with the tips.

"Don't move," the tall one on the left said. "Resistance is not smart."

"Oh, okay. Hadn't thought about that."

A shadow covered her vision. Reflex caused her to blink. Then something filled her mouth. She fought back, but they subdued her arms.

Machiavelli's thick gloves were rancid. He had placed at least three fingers in her open mouth and dragged her across the floor by the roof of her mouth, her front teeth taking on much of the pressure. She kicked her feet to relieve a modicum of pressure off her mouth. If only the men holding her arms would lift higher, but somehow they added to weighing her down.

She clenched her jaw muscles and clamped down hard in an attempt to close her mouth and sever his fingers, but the gloves were too thick.

Then it was over. Something very cold was under her. His fingers came out of her mouth, leaving behind the horrible taste of rubber and mucus. She gagged and hated the image of weakness it portrayed.

The grime on her shirt and pants from hiding behind the garbage bins at the back of the Chinese restaurant still reeked and chilled her on the metal table as the vegetable oil seemed to conduct the cold right through her skin and into her bones.

She turned toward Machiavelli, ready to leap off the table and attack him, consequences be damned, but a bucket of water hit her face. She gasped as the liquid dripped from her upper body and then moaned at the pain in her cheek. She blinked rapidly and wiped her eyes.

Machiavelli walked over to another counter and flicked several switches on the wall until the room was bathed in light from strong overhead bulbs. The guards on either side of her stayed close enough to touch her hips.

The small room had a sink and cupboards along one wall. Like an Italian cappuccino maker, a large machine sat on the counter beside Machiavelli, thick wires protruding from each side. A small table to her right was covered with a black cloth. On the cloth were various implements and what looked like tools of torture.

"You stink, Sarah." Machiavelli turned around, the gloves gone. "Thought the water would help, but now you smell like a drowned rat. Fucking pathetic, really."

With everything in her core, she wanted so badly to leap off the steel table and drive his face into the corner of the wall, mouth open so the corner could divide his teeth and rip open his gums.

"What is this?" she managed to ask. "What's next?"

Machiavelli raised his hands. "This is the basement of my funeral home. We cremate people here." He turned and tapped what looked like the cappuccino machine beside him. "This is an embalming unit." He pointed at the table she had spied a moment ago. "Those tools help us find the vein, then using these tubes, we fill dead bodies with embalming fluid. Quite simple, really."

"Why are we here?" she asked.

"Because you're dead." He wagged a finger at her. "And just like your sister's voice in your head, you're dead, but I can still hear you. Fascinating, isn't it?"

"It's fascinating if you're deranged."

His face turned serious. "Are you?"

"Absolutely."

"Thought so."

"Then what are we waiting for?" she yelled. "Let's get on with this shit."

"We are waiting for Niles and Fletcher to join us. Niles is the one who will perform your cremation."

"Oh, am I to be cremated alive? Wait, isn't Niles dead yet? That's your plan, isn't it?"

He nodded and moved closer. The men on either side of her didn't move an inch.

"Cremation is such a cost-effective way to remove our garbage, our used-up girls. Did you know that before the year 2000, only about twenty-five percent of the dead were cremated? By 2017, the number will be as high as fifty percent."

A man stepped into view. It was Fletcher Aldrich from yesterday at Nathan Phillips Square.

"We'll only be a moment longer," Fletcher said. He met Sarah's eyes. "Then you will be pushed into that." He pointed. "And cremated alive. Look at our security. We have twenty men upstairs. There's absolutely no chance of escape this time, Sarah Roberts. No chance."

A pit the size of a football settled in her stomach. There had to be another way. This couldn't be over. But how often had she seen the end and lived through it? Vivian had to see this coming.

"You murdered my brother and then my father," Fletcher said. "I will see you roast alive for that."

Machiavelli stepped into view beside the table. "You made my men ruin my expensive car. Gonna cost you for that, too."

"Well, I'll work hard to pay that back once I'm dead. Smart play killing me, asshole. Smart play."

Machiavelli looked up at Fletcher with a fake smile. "Always the joker."

"I try."

He moved close and hovered over her face. "You're pathetic. What made you think this would work, whatever it is you think you've done? Fletcher here, along with Mason, will burn you to ashes. Sarah Roberts will have disappeared." He stood and moved away. "I'm doing you a favor. No long trial. No prison sentence."

"Gee, thanks."

Vivian? Anything here? Could use some help.

"Is Niles ready?" Machiavelli asked Fletcher.

"He'll be in in a sec. Bandaging his hand."

"His hand?" Sarah asked.

"He has lost two fingers in an industrial accident," Fletcher said. "One has to be careful."

"Does he know about his wife?" Sarah asked.

"He knows you killed her." Fletcher's face was deadpan.

"Why did he lose his fingers?"

"Because he fucked up," Fletcher snapped. "We have rules. He violated them. It's his fault that Vanessa escaped and wanted to kill herself in the first place."

"He allowed her to escape," Sarah said. Then Vivian provided the rest, and Sarah spoke as she became aware of the information. It warmed her on the inside to hear Vivian's voice so close. "He used his key to open the back door."

Fletcher looked at her sidelong. "How would you know something like that?"

"Friends in high places."

"Smart-ass comments might work well on the street, but it only makes life difficult down here."

"Agreed. Life has been punishing down here on this steel table all covered in water. But you know what they say about looking on the bright side?"

"The bright side? There's a bright side for you here?"

"Well, no, just thought it sounded good." She shrugged. "Needed something to say."

"While we wait for Niles," Machiavelli said. "Let me ask you something, Sarah. You're aware of the consistency of beach sand?"

She remained motionless, glaring at him.

"That is cremated human ashes. When your body is

cremated, it's not like on TV. When people release the ashes into the ocean or a river, they float because they're light and fluffy. In real life, ashes resemble beach sand. Heavy and thick. Did you know that?"

"Can't say I've had the opportunity to come by that information."

"Cremation costs about three grand on average, but a burial can run upward of eight thousand. Crazy, eh?"

"Are you in training for employee of the month?"

"There's even a company," he continued, ignoring her, "that will put your ashes into bullets. It's called Holy Smoke. Another one, for the right price, sends your ashes to outer space. Isn't that fantastic?"

Sarah leaned up on the table but was slammed back down so hard by the man on her left that her shoulder blade stung briefly again.

"Tell her, Niles," Machiavelli said as the detective entered the room. "Tell her how you let us down."

Detective Niles Mason's eyes were bloodshot with black bags under them as if he hadn't slept in days. Specks of blood spread across the bridge of his nose and his jaw. When he moved closer to the steel table, Sarah saw the reason for the blood on his face. His left hand had a mound of red-stained bandages piled on it. His arm ended in what looked like a very large Q-Tip. Niles was as pale as a ghost, and his hair was unkempt, shoved back as if he didn't have the use of gel today.

"Sarah," he said, his tone wavering, weak, like that of a scared eight-year-old boy in a schoolyard facing off a bully. "You have caused a lot," he paused, swallowed, then said, "a lot of trouble." He held up his bandaged hand. "Because I let

Vanessa go free, they took my wife. I needed to kill Detective Simmons to make things right. But that wasn't enough. I needed to take you out, too. I gave you the gun in that parking lot to make it look justified. But you got away." His eyes moved to Machiavelli for support. The councilor nodded. "I have one more person to kill to make things right."

"No way," Fletcher said, pushing forward and shoving Detective Mason out of the way. "Sarah's mine. After what she did to my family, I get to kill her."

"Men," Machiavelli said to the guards on either side of her. "Leave us. Guard the outer door. No one leaves this room until I say so. And let no one in. I don't care what you hear in here; no one comes in. Got it?"

In unison, the guards barked out their acknowledgment and walked away, disappearing around the corner. A moment later, a door in the other room closed firmly.

"Now that we're alone," Machiavelli said. "We can begin —"

"When I said I have someone else to kill, I wasn't talking about Sarah," Mason said under his breath.

"What?" Fletcher snarled.

Even with her head turned sideways, Sarah saw the weapon in Mason's good hand. Fletcher looked down as the weapon discharged, and then his body vibrated as the bullet entered his abdomen. Sarah's body went rigid on the table. The trajectory of the bullet could've passed through Fletcher and into her, but it didn't.

Mason raised the weapon and fired again. This time only the noise made her jerk.

Fletcher stumbled backward, his hands covering the

stomach wound as if that alone would keep the blood in. He faltered another step, bumped her steel gurney, and fell over her legs.

She screamed out as her knees were pushed into the gurney in a way they weren't supposed to bend, and then the pressure was gone an instant later as Fletcher slipped off the table and hit the floor with a satisfying thump.

Somewhere upstairs, a commotion started. A gun fired.

What the hell is that now?

Mason looked at Sarah, his eyes devoid of life as if something dead had crawled inside his skull and rooted behind his optic nerve.

"Fletcher should have never allowed his brother free rein in that house in Orillia. Too many innocents died there. I should've stopped him years ago, but I was weak. I'm not weak anymore."

Someone clapped their hands.

To her left, Machiavelli stood beside the steel gurney, clapping, smiling.

"Well done, Mason. You've paid your dues. You're back in." Machiavelli walked around to the head of the gurney, unlocked something out of sight, and started pushing Sarah toward the other side of the room. "You're officially on the payroll again, Mason. See, Sarah, as I told you earlier, Detective Niles Mason is the one who has the order to execute you. He gets to do the honors."

Sarah made to jump from the gurney, but it was no use as Mason's gun pressed against her temple. His wounded arm wrapped around her head, resting on her chest.

More noise from upstairs. Someone clomped by, their footfalls heavy and determined.

"Don't try to get up," he whispered. "Please don't make me destroy your pretty face."

"What's next?" Sarah asked, looking down at his roaming hand. "Dinner and a movie? Or did I miss that part?"

"You are a strange one, Sarah," Machiavelli said. "Too bad you weren't on my side. You'd humor me with your wise-ass mouth."

"Somehow, I don't think that would be the only thing my mouth would be used for if I was on your side."

"Finally, the wise-ass smartens up." Machiavelli stopped pushing the gurney as it bumped into something. He looked down at her. "Too bad there isn't more time. I would love to taste a woman with so much anger in her. Although you'd have to shower that smell off first." He moved away and pushed a button. A small door that resembled a tiny garage rose to reveal the inside of a cremation chamber, the flames already lit.

"You want to join me for tea in Hell?" Sarah asked, surprised her voice didn't waver. "There's a seat at the Devil's Café open for you."

"No, I think not. You and hundreds of women before you have met these flames. My crematorium has taken so many women. You're just another number. A necessary one, but just a number. Goodbye, Sarah."

He walked out of view. She arched her head back to see what he was doing, but Mason was in the way. Behind her, he worked on something under the gurney. Then the steel slab moved. It slid closer to the open maw of the fires. Panic rose, and her throat tightened.

Then it all stopped at the sound of a gun. Mason's arm

lifted off her. She spun around to see what was happening as more noise came from upstairs. Someone was knocking on the outer door now.

She arched her head back.

Upside down, she watched as Mason fired again and again into Machiavelli. When he fell, Machiavelli bumped into a table on wheels and spilled the tools onto the tile floor in a huge racket.

Mason waited until Machiavelli stopped twitching before he took his eyes off him and turned back to Sarah.

He trudged over to her, the look on his face one of acceptance now. He actually appeared calm, resolute.

"Taking Samantha was their mistake," he said. "Beat me, hurt me, but touch my wife—no, they went too far." He looked down at his shoes and shook his head as tears fell from his eyes. "They went too far. And now it's all over."

Someone knocked on a door again. What sounded like Detective Diner's voice yelled Mason's name.

"I called my partner here so she could do the cleanup. I want you to tell her everything."

What was he thinking? That he would die down here? Or kill himself? Sarah had been around death so often that when Fletcher and Machiavelli were killed in front of her, she didn't feel a thing except for maybe relief. But Mason had helped Vanessa escape and then lost his wife. He wasn't entirely to blame here.

"You tell her yourself, Mason," Sarah said. "Wait for her to come in."

"There's a black book with every person's name in it. Machiavelli usually manages it, but it was removed recently. They thought Vanessa had taken it, but she didn't. Find the black book. Every crime, every victim, every violator to cross The Club's path is in that book."

Someone banged on the door harder this time. Diner's voice was clear. She identified herself and explained that she was coming in.

"The black book might be at the warehouse, but I can't be sure. Take these." He held out what looked like little ID cards. "With these, they'll let you in." He gently slipped them inside her pants pocket. "I've done all I can."

A door burst open in the other room.

Mason raised the gun to his chin and squeezed the trigger without hesitation.

Sarah shut her eyes and turned away, but not in time. The top of Mason's head lifted off in a small puff, his hair billowing as air blew it up from the inside of his head. Before closing her eyes, she saw the blood splatter on the ceiling above him.

"Gun!" someone yelled from the other room.

"No shit," Sarah yelled back.

Detective Diner moved into view. After pushing the button to close the door to the fires of cremation, she turned to look at Sarah, completely ignoring the body of her partner at her feet.

"I didn't see my car out front."

"Yeah, well, we're going to have to talk about that."

Chapter 27

"THIS IS HOW THEY dispose of so many victims," Sarah said in an attempt to explain what had happened at the funeral home.

"No." Detective Diner raised a finger at Sarah. "Don't talk right now. I don't want to hear your voice."

Police officers swarmed throughout the funeral home like angry bees searching out the queen. They had entered through the front door, Diner leading the way with a warrant that her partner had already requested. She brought a contingent of fifty officers and a division of Toronto's ETF. Two fire trucks were parked out front, and several ambulances were on standby. During the assault, only one officer was shot in the lower leg by Machiavelli's men.

Officers entering the funeral home had encountered little to no resistance from the twenty-two men in the waiting room and surrounding premises upstairs. According to officers reporting to Diner, only two people had been killed other than the two city councilors and Niles in the cremation room. It was clear early on what happened in the funeral home's basement. Maybe that was why Detective Diner hadn't asked for Sarah's version yet.

Diner handcuffed Sarah and whispered, "How does it feel now that the tables have turned?"

Diner brought Sarah upstairs and asked two officers to guard her in the waiting room.

Detective Diner dropped onto the sofa in the waiting room beside Sarah a half-hour later.

"You want to fill me in?" She turned to look at Sarah. "What the hell happened here? What's going on? Why is my partner dead?"

"There are men in our society that want more from women …" Sarah started.

Diner scrunched her eyes and shot her head back. "What?" she said in an exasperated tone.

"Let me explain. I'm still learning all the facts myself. These men are running something that used to be called a Torture Garden."

"A Torture Garden? You don't mean the TG that started in London a few decades ago, do you?"

"As far as I know, yes." They were bringing Mason's body upstairs. Sarah waited until they passed so she could have Diner's full attention. "How would you know about the Torture Garden?" Sarah asked.

"I worked a case a few years back regarding a misper at Buddies in Bad Times Theatre in Toronto. My investigation brought me to the Torture Garden's doorstep. I researched them, checked to see if their paperwork was in order, and left it at that. Based on our laws here in Ontario, the Torture

Garden is legal. They're in major cities across the globe like London, Athens, and Moscow."

"What these men were doing," Sarah said, "was bringing a whole new meaning to torture. They took what the TG had done and added to it."

Diner got up from the sofa. "How do you know all this?"

"My sister."

"You mean your dead sister?"

Sarah nodded.

"You know, Sarah, those cuffs are on you because you're going downtown to be formally charged for the crimes you've committed over the past few days. The murder of Vanessa Simmons, Joel and Belinda, and Aldrich senior in the cancer hospital, to name a few. If you're thinking of pleading insanity and talking wild stories about a dead sister speaking to you, then the schizo defense might work. But it'll be a year or two process, and there's no way a judge would allow bail. Not with what you've done."

"I've got a surprise for you, Detective."

"What's that?"

"Not yet," Sarah said, shaking her head. "Not yet."

"I'm pissed about my car."

"I know. But there's more."

"More? What are you talking about, more?"

"The warehouse." Sarah met Diner's eyes.

"Okay, I'll bite. What warehouse?"

"These councilors own a warehouse. Inside, they have kidnapped girls being held captive. That's where the real torture happens. When the girls succumb to their injuries, they're brought here and cremated, never to be heard from again. Aren't you ever curious about the staggering number of missing people, especially young girls, who never turn up? And there are people like Detective Simmons who get caught up with this consortium because of the money. He felt he was once removed, but he wasn't. They watched him like a hawk. One mistake, and he had to pay with his daughter. It was Mason who saved Vanessa. But then Mason had to pay with his wife. It's no wonder he lost it in there and shot the men responsible for the murder of his wife."

"Okay," Diner put her hands on her hips. "I've heard you. Now listen to me." She cleared her throat. "I don't believe in the other side. There are no ghosts, no boogeymen, and no God. But I do believe in evil men. So say you're right about this warehouse. Where is it, and how could we build a case around it if the dead councilors downstairs ran it? Who is left to arrest?"

"There are more powerful men out there who help run it."

"Really, I'm curious." Diner leaned forward until she was almost nose to nose with Sarah. "How do you *know* all this shit?"

"I told you. Vivian, my dead sister."

They locked eyes. Diner blinked and backed away.

"You won't lighten up and tell me the truth about your source? Right?"

"That is the truth."

"I'll make you a deal."

Sarah nodded and crossed her legs. "Go ahead. This ought to be interesting."

"Prove to me Vivian exists. Prove there is an other side, and I will believe everything you say to the point that you knew what you were doing from the start."

"What are you saying?" Sarah asked, her head slanted to the side. "I walk if Vivian's real?"

"I didn't say that. I said I would believe you. I would think of you in a different light. As if you're on our side and not an insane vigilante."

"I'll think about it."

"What?"

"I said I would think about it. But first, you have to take me to the warehouse."

"The warehouse?"

"Yes. Right now. Because they haven't heard that Machiavelli and Fletcher are dead. Operations are in full swing as we speak. Once they discover what happened here, they'll be shutting everything down and cleaning the place up until they regroup and find a new spot."

"I would never take you there. They'd take my badge. You're a civilian. And you're out of your mind."

"You will take me there. And you'll just take me alone. A bunch of cops would spook them. But we have to do it now."

Diner straightened her jacket and stared down at Sarah. "You've got some balls."

"It's the only way."

Diner looked her up and down. "You're crazy."

"I will do something for you," Sarah whispered.

"What?" Diner leaned in. "Say again," she said, sarcasm in her words. "Didn't hear you."

It was clear Detective Diner had lost her patience and allowed anger to influence her decisions.

"I will tell you what happened to your ..." Sarah paused and smiled gently. "I will explain what happened to your brother."

Diner gasped and stood back. Color filled her cheeks. She mumbled something, then took another step back.

"How dare you?" Diner hissed. "How fucking dare you?" Diner grabbed the cop guarding Sarah by the forearm. "Get her out of here. Place her in my cruiser. Then stay outside the car." The cop was nodding. "Do not talk to this woman. Do not listen to a word she says." Diner looked at another officer guarding Sarah. "Can you both do that?"

They nodded. "Absolutely, Detective."

"Good. Go." Diner glared at Sarah. "Get her out of my sight."

Chapter 28

THE CRUISER WAS HOT. Too hot to be stuck inside. The smell from the Chinese restaurant hadn't dissipated, and in this heat, it worsened.

All the windows were rolled up, and the car wasn't turned on, so no air conditioning alleviated the sun as it beat in through the windshield hot enough to melt the grease embedded in her shirt.

She yelled to the officers standing outside that this was cruel and unusual punishment, but as instructed, they didn't pay any attention to her. After five minutes, the only air she was getting was through her mouth as she breathed slowly and evenly.

Furtive glances back to the entrance of the funeral home were fruitless. Detective Diner would come out when she was done and not a second sooner.

In the quiet of the vehicle, Sarah closed her eyes and

listened for Vivian.

You out there?

Nothing came to her.

That's great. Thanks.

Sarah jumped as the car door ripped open, and Diner dropped inside. She turned the car on, and the air conditioner began blowing blessed cool air into the back. Sarah breathed in deeply. Her shirt was soaked through with sweat in the short time she had been in the car, and now it gave her the chills as the air cooled it.

Diner turned around and placed her arm on the back of the seat.

"What the fuck are you trying to do?" Diner asked.

"Finish this case."

"And? What was that about my brother?"

"That was to help you believe in my sister and, ultimately, the other side."

She threw her hands up in exasperation. "Say I believe in the other side. Let's go all the way and say I believe in everything you represent. What has that got to do with my brother?"

"Start driving." Sarah shivered from the cold involuntarily. "I will direct you."

"To what?"

"To your brother."

Diner didn't talk for a full minute, and Sarah wasn't about to interrupt her thoughts.

"Where is he?" she asked.

Sarah shook her head. "No. You drive there. Then we go to the warehouse."

"No way."

"Once inside the warehouse, you will see everything you need to see to make all the busts necessary. You can close these assholes down for good."

"And how do we get inside?"

"Leave that to me."

"Ohhh, you love all the control, don't you? Like this is your show, and I'm just a guest."

Sarah glanced out the window and watched as another body was removed from the funeral home. It wasn't often that bodies were taken *out* of funeral homes in this manner.

"Then what?" Diner asked. "I arrest you for all your crimes, and that's it? You explain to the judge how much help you gave me, hoping it'll reduce your sentence? Or are you still going for the insanity plea?"

"One thing at a time. We can deal with that later. There's something you need to get at the warehouse."

"What's that?"

Sarah turned from the window. "There's a black book. This book lists the names of all the people who tortured the victims and every victim ever to set foot in the warehouse. Get the black book, and you have the case of the century. The problem is, this black book has city councilors, powerful judges, mafia types, all the way down to rich men visiting Toronto and wanting a little fun."

"That sort of thing doesn't bother me. I don't care how powerful you are. If you broke the law, I will arrest you."

"Great. Then start driving. The black book is in the warehouse today. Tomorrow it won't be."

Diner turned back in her seat and faced forward. After a moment, she put the unmarked cruiser in gear and drove them off the funeral home's property.

"Where to?" she asked.

"The warehouse is—"

"No," Diner cut her off. "Where is my brother?"

"Take the 401 until you hit Brock Road near Pickering. Head north on Brock."

"Wow, I'm impressed. You know a lot about this area for an American."

"I'm only repeating what my sister has told me."

Diner's eyes met hers in the rearview mirror, then looked away only enough to watch the road.

Sarah stared at the passing scenery and hoped they weren't getting to the warehouse too late.

If they were, a man would be leaving with the black book. If he took it, the book would leave the country by tomorrow. It would never be located again.

Maybe that's why Vivian told me to ask Aaron for a ride to the airport.

Chapter 29

As Diner turned north on Brock Road, Sarah watched the mall pass by on her right.

"Turn in here," Sarah instructed.

Diner hit her indicator and turned into the mall.

"Park by the Walmart."

Sarah directed Diner until they were backed into a spot. Once parked, Diner left the car running and turned in her seat.

"So, what is this?" Diner asked.

"The reason you're in law enforcement."

"Oh, really. And why is that?"

Sarah looked down at her legs. It was odd knowing so much personal information about the detective. It made Sarah feel invasive. But it was necessary.

"Your sixteenth birthday. Brad, your fraternal twin brother, argued with your father."

Sarah heard Diner adjust herself in the front seat.

"Your father had been in a car accident," Sarah said.

"No," Diner broke in. "Correction. My brother killed that woman."

Sarah looked up and met Diner's eyes. Behind them, she saw a struggle. Diner was fighting back the tears, but the tears were winning.

"Your father was driving," Sarah whispered.

"That's impossible. My brother admitted it. He confessed. He went to jail for it."

"He did the time," Sarah nodded. "But he was a youth under the Young Offenders Act. The charges were dangerous driving, failing to remain, vehicular manslaughter, etc. Basically a hit-and-run, but a woman was killed. He got probation and a year in a youth center. Shortly after the trial, your father died. Alcoholism caught up with his liver, his body."

Tears bubbled up under Diner's eyes, then dropped off her face as the painful memories surfaced. "How in the hell could you know all this?" She used the tips of her fingers to mash the tears from her eyes. "I checked years later. The criminal record was purged when Brad turned eighteen."

"Your father was drunk that day," Sarah said. "He had taken Brad out to teach him how to be a man, but Brad didn't want to drink. When your father hit that woman with his car, he panicked and left the scene, but a neighbor wrote his plate number down. By the time the police arrived, he still hadn't sobered up. He said Brad was learning how to drive. It was an accident. At first, your brother denied it, but your father convinced him that one year wasn't a lot. If good old dad had to take the fall, charged as an adult, well, you know better than me how that would go."

Diner turned away and lowered her head, fumbling with something in her lap.

"When my brother got out, he never came to the house." Diner's shoulders hitched. She swallowed. "He never came to my father's funeral."

"You always wondered what happened that day. Why they argued. Your search for the truth started there. Your mother never spoke of it because she didn't know any better. As far as she was concerned, Brad was a murderer."

Diner nodded. "My alcoholic father ruined our family, then died."

"Have you forgiven your father?" Sarah asked.

Diner watched a car drive by, searching for a parking spot as if she didn't hear Sarah's question. "How sure are you that my dad was driving?"

"Sure enough that I brought you to see your brother. Ask him yourself."

She swung around in her seat like someone had jerked on her head with a rope. "He's here? Right now?"

Sarah nodded slowly.

"I looked him up," Diner exclaimed. "I hunted for him. After he got out of jail, he disappeared. How could you find him?"

Sarah gave her a *come-on, really*, look and said, "Brad isn't Brad Diner anymore."

"What's his name?" she nearly shouted.

"Marcus Appleby."

"Marcus? What?" Now she was screaming. Then she started to laugh through her tears. "Who the hell calls himself Marcus Appleby?"

Sarah nodded at the dash. "What time is it?"

Diner wiped her eyes and bent closer to the clock, still uttering a few choking laughs, or sobs, Sarah wasn't quite sure.

"It's seven minutes after two."

"Roll the window down on my side."

Diner did, but it only went halfway.

"In three minutes, at 2:10, Brad or Marcus will enter that black Camaro two cars over. I'd suggest you get out and say something to him."

"What? But I haven't seen him since we were sixteen. What would I say? What am I supposed to—" she stopped, then narrowed her eyes. "You researched me. You looked me up, and now you're making fun of my pain." Her face turned serious. "There's no way in hell that you could know all that. This is a prank, isn't it?"

"I agree. There's no way in hell. When Marcus walks by, you will have no choice but to embrace your twin brother and the fact that there is something to this dead sister talk of mine."

Diner checked her watch. She opened her car door and got out, leaving the car running and the air going full. Ten seconds later, she stuck her head back in.

"In one minute, I will see my brother. Or I will make it my life's mission to cause you as much pain and sorrow as possible for the rest of my life."

She slammed the door so hard the cruiser rocked back and forth. Diner moved to the front of the cruiser and leaned on the hood.

They waited.

A woman walked by pushing a stroller, a balloon

attached to the handle. Beside her, a boy about the age of four cried as she schooled him on his behavior. Two teenagers who were supposed to be in school ran by, one clutching a skateboard.

They waited.

Then Diner pushed off the cruiser, walked around to her door, yanked it open, and dropped back in the car.

"I can't believe I let this go on as far as I did." She put the car in gear. "And to think, a fucking psychic murderer had me wound up, all ready to—"

"Marina Sue Diner!" Sarah yelled. "Shut the fuck up!"

The car stopped with a jerk.

"Do not move this car," Sarah shouted. "Look to your right."

Diner fixed her gaze out the passenger window and stared at the man walking toward the black Camaro. Slowly, she put the car back into park.

"I can't believe it," came out of her mouth, barely above a whisper.

"If you don't get out of the car now," Sarah said. "You'll miss him."

Diner froze. Her eyes darted to his face, his pants, and the little boy hugging his father's leg.

"I can't believe—" she started.

"Excuse me, sir?" Sarah shouted out her window. "Do you have a moment?"

"Sarah!" Diner whispered in a breathy yelp.

Marcus frowned as he opened the back seat of the Camaro and placed his son inside. He put the Walmart bags in the front passenger seat and faced the unmarked cruiser.

"Do I know you?" he asked. He narrowed his eyes and

turned his head sideways with a conspiratorial grin. "Did John put you up to this?"

"I'm afraid it's not a joke," Sarah said. "I need one minute of your time."

Marcus didn't come closer. He leaned down to get a look at the driver but stayed by his vehicle two spots over.

"Looks like the cops to me," he said, his tone brusque now. "What do you want?"

"The driver wants to have a word."

Diner opened the door. She got out and walked around the trunk. Sarah watched her progress. A realization swept across his face when Diner stopped in front of Marcus. Maybe it had something to do with being twins. Both of them recognized each other within seconds after almost two decades.

"Little Marina?" he managed to say. "Is it really you?"

Detective Diner shot out her arms and hugged him, unable to speak as sobs overwhelmed her. Marcus held her. They leaned against the Camaro for a few minutes as they tried to get themselves under control.

Questions poured out of both of them. Sarah watched the reunion with growing dread. Someone was going to inform the men at the torture warehouse that Machiavelli and Fletcher were dead. They would shut down soon.

But this was necessary. Detective Diner had to be sold.

And what a good way to sell her, Sis. I love this stuff.

Sarah wondered if this was what she should be doing instead of all the dangerous stuff.

Maybe we should spend time bringing people together like this instead of vigilantism.

Vivian whispered that there would be plenty of time to

do the lovey-dovey tasks when Sarah was older and more feeble. Not now while she was still able to fight.

Great!

"Detective Diner?" Sarah interrupted. By this point, Marcus had introduced his three-year-old boy and offered Diner to come for dinner to meet his wife. They both agreed it had been too long. "Detective?"

"Yeah?" she turned toward Sarah, her eyes bloodshot. "What?"

"We have to go."

"Where?"

"A certain warehouse. Not much time."

Diner looked at the pavement, then back up into her brother's eyes. They spoke of seeing each other this weekend and exchanged numbers.

Two minutes later, Diner was back behind the wheel and turning onto Brock Road.

"You okay?" Sarah asked.

"Yeah. Let's do this, and then I need a week off. I need to reconnect. I still can't believe it." She shook her head. "I just can't believe it."

"Get back on the 401 and head toward Scarborough. Turn north on McCowan Road. The warehouse we're going to is five minutes north off of Nugget."

Diner looked back at her through her rearview mirror. "You sure about this? Just you and me? No backup?"

The refreshing feel of the detective's voice sent waves of calm through Sarah. Diner was on her side, even if it was temporarily.

"It's the only way. They have too many cameras, magnetic door locks, and security posted outside. From what my sister told me, I understand that they even have security posted at several places along the street, watching vehicles from over a mile's distance each way. One word, and the place gets locked down. If they can't get out because of a raid, there's a large cage, like a panic room, in a hiding place under the building. It's soundproof. In the event of an emergency, the victims are to be herded in there. If all the operators are arrested, anyone inside the panic room will be left to die of starvation as there would be no one to let them out." Sarah closed her eyes, looking inward, listening. "Only two people know the code to that panic room, and they're both dead. The men in the warehouse don't know that yet."

"Wow, you really know your stuff."

"Most of this I just learned as I spoke it. Trust me. My sister has her own way of doling information out. Pisses me off most times, but everything always works out. In the end, it all works out."

Diner looked at her again, but Sarah averted her eyes.

She probably heard the uncertainty in my voice.

Chapter 30

Detective Marina Diner drove past the warehouse without slowing to get a look at the building.

"I don't see any guards posted outside," Diner said. "You know, something's telling me this is not a good idea."

Sarah adjusted herself as the handcuffs were cutting into the flesh of her wrists. And now she had to pee so bad her leg wouldn't stop bouncing.

"Pull in up here and turn around. Before we get back, listen to me and listen well because I'll only have time to say this once."

Diner slowed to perform the U-turn.

"I'm listening."

"We're going in as guests."

"We are? Whose guests?"

"Diner," Sarah said, her voice low. "Listen."

Marina nodded, then pulled back onto Nugget Road,

heading back the way they had come.

"You're taking me in to abuse me."

Diner's head shot up to look in the mirror.

"Play along, Detective. I'm handcuffed. They will understand this. They will know my face already. And they know who you are."

"How?"

"Because of Mason."

Diner slowed the vehicle to pull into the warehouse's parking lot.

"You're going to ask for a medical room," Sarah said.

"What's that?"

"No idea, but I'm sure we're about to find out." Sarah studied the building, trying to find their security, but no one was in sight. "Park up here."

Diner pulled in beside a BMW and turned the car off.

"Now what?" she asked.

"Leave your weapon in the car."

"No way."

"They'll frisk you. You have no choice. Hide your cell phone, though. Take me in as your prisoner. Ask for the medical room. Lock the door behind you. Then call for backup. Got it?"

"Is that your master plan? All this way, and that's how you expect to bust these guys from the inside?"

"That's all I have."

"How do we get inside?"

Sarah didn't get a chance to respond as Diner's door was ripped open. A large, bearded man in a black suit stood by the door, a machine gun draped subtly under his suit jacket, the tip sticking out by his thigh.

"Step out of the car, Detective Diner."

A radio crackled nearby.

Diner snuck a glance at Sarah, then got out. "You got a permit for that thing, Mr. Turner?" she asked.

Not the best way to infiltrate them, Diner.

"Step aside," Turner ordered.

Behind three different cars, men wearing the same suit as Turner stood with machine guns.

Why does it always have to look so hopeless?

Her leg bounced faster as her bladder threatened to release.

Then her door opened.

"Sarah. Exit the car."

A slimmer man, clean-cut and handsome, wearing the same suit with the same large anti-aircraft gun slung over his shoulder, held the door open for her.

She edged sideways along the car seat, set her feet on the concrete, and pushed off. He guided her around the car to stand beside Diner.

Sarah counted seven men watching them now. The radio crackled again. Turner touched something on his belt, then touched his earpiece as he listened.

When he removed his finger, he focused his eyes on Diner.

"You're alone?" His tone wasn't as much a question as it was a surprise. Like, *Really? Why the hell would you come here alone?*

Diner nodded. "Just the two of us." She sang the words in a carefree tone.

That's how you play this, Diner. Cool.

"Why?" Turner asked.

"She's mine," Diner nodded at Sarah. "I'm taking her to the medical room." Diner stopped talking, adjusted her weight, then said, "And when we're done, ashes to ashes, right?"

Okay, Diner, talk less now. I'm not enjoying this anymore.

"Invites?" he asked. "Pass cards? Anything?"

"In my pocket," Sarah said, thrusting her hip out slightly.

Diner frowned. Turner offered a brief smile, then it was gone.

The detective eased her finger inside Sarah's pocket, pulled out the two ID cards Mason had given her in the funeral home's basement, and then handed them to Turner.

He examined them and nodded. "They're cleared. IDs are in order." He walked away. "Take them inside. Make sure medical room number two is clean and prepared." When he was ten feet away, he turned back and looked at them over his shoulder. "Ladies, if you will follow me."

They started forward. The instant Turner spoke, the seven guards returned to their hiding places. Only the handsome one followed them to the front door of the warehouse.

Turner held the door open as they entered, Diner in the lead. Sarah hoped she remembered to bring her cell phone.

Once inside a two-door chamber that puffed air on them like a bomb scan at an airport, they entered a search area akin to airport security.

Three guards moved in and frisked Diner first. When they finished the manual search, one of the men scanned her body meticulously with an electronic wand. They only pulled out her cell phone, but then they offered it back to her when they were done.

"No weapons, no wires, no listening devices, nothing. She's clean."

Turner nodded, then jerked his head toward Sarah.

The same routine was performed on her, but his hands were more probing and certainly rougher. At one point, she thought she would knee him in the nose when his face was too close to her crotch during the inspection.

The guard nodded. "Clean."

At the top of the door behind them, a large, rectangular silver block engaged a magnetic lock. Nothing was getting through that door unless the power was cut.

"Can we hurry this along," Sarah said. "Gotta pee."

Neither guard saw the humor, their faces remaining unchanged.

"Tough crowd tonight."

Diner gave her a stern look.

"Sorry," Sarah whispered. "Just trying to work on the tension in this room."

After a minute's wait, the door in front of them—a bank vault door—clicked as if it was on a timer and creaked open. When it was fully open, the inside of the waiting area was exposed.

Must've cost a lot of money for this kind of security.

They were heralded into a waiting room where champagne and wine were being served. On Sarah's left, four men in business suits crowded a small bar where a woman in a bikini served drinks.

Diner led them to a red leather sofa against a back wall with room for two. A well-dressed man in shiny black shoes approached her and whispered that the medical room would be available within minutes.

Sarah didn't recognize anyone in the waiting area. A quick count came to over a dozen men milling around, drinking, chatting, and snacking on crackers and small olives stabbed with toothpicks. The furniture was expensive leather, Italian tile on the floor, and paintings of women in various poses adorned the walls.

Naked women meandered throughout the men, offering snacks and beverages. One wore a dog collar with a chain dangling past her hips. Another wore a leather facial mask, and one blonde girl who didn't look a day over twenty crawled on the floor, a leash attached to the collar on her neck. In a far corner, a woman wore heels that had to be seven inches high, her toes coming to a point at the floor. She held a leash with a man attached. She ordered the man to heel, then started to walk, stopped, whipped his buttocks with a cat-o-nine tails, and barked another command.

A few men glanced over but paid little attention to the act guaranteed to be found in a sex circus emporium.

Diner's uneasiness oozed off her as she grew fidgety beside Sarah. A glance this way, a sudden jerk of the head that way. Sarah hoped Diner could hold it together long enough to get inside the room and call for help.

A door opened across from them, and a man exited. He was slipping on a suit jacket with a wide grin. Behind him, Sarah saw a woman tied to the wall, her legs spread wide like she was caught in the middle of a jumping jack and suspended that way. Her purple face and bleeding mouth told Sarah half the story of what went on in that room. The other half of the story was about the item suspended from the woman's vagina and the blood dripping from it. Red and purplish lacerations from the man's belt rippled across her thighs and shins.

Then the door closed, cutting off the sight.

Another woman screeched from down the hallway. It sounded like the high-pitched wail of a dying rabbit.

Diner leaned close to Sarah and whispered, "This is awful. Sarah, I'm scared here. This was a bad idea."

"I'm scared, too," Sarah said under her breath.

The man in the suit with the shiny black shoes who had just told Diner her room would be ready soon approached the man who had just come out of the room in front of them.

"How was Delilah?" he asked. "Did she meet all your expectations?"

"Yes, but she'll need a month or two to heal," the man said, an ugly smirk on his face. "Sorry about that. Got carried away this time. I'll pay the extra needed for her recuperation."

"That's no problem." The suited man spoke as if his voice was made of silk. "That's what they're here for. As long as you've had your amusement, then we're all happy. Even Delilah is happy to serve."

He guided the man to where the girl with the dog collar and chain placed a drink in his hand.

The girl met Sarah's eyes for a brief moment. In that second, Sarah saw the fear, the humiliation, and the disgust for the people around her. This girl didn't want to be here as much as a concentration camp survivor didn't want to stay in their camp. But Sarah thought she detected something else in the girl's eyes. Hopelessness. The girl believed there was no way out. This was her life now, at least what was left of it.

And all thanks to someone like Detective Timothy Simmons.

That's why Mason let Vanessa leave through the back door.

The man with the shiny shoes stepped in front of them.

"Your room is ready."

Diner and Sarah followed him down a short hall where they passed two other men exiting rooms.

At the end of the hall, a door opened into an area that looked like the kind a brain surgeon would perform a twelve-hour operation in.

Two tables littered with surgical tools sat in the center of the room. A metal bed covered in a plastic sheet was pushed up against the tables of tools. Under it was a large drainage grate where Sarah assumed all the victim's blood would seep out of the room.

The man shut the door as he left them and locked it from the outside. They looked at each other and expelled air at the same time.

"Holy shit," Diner said.

"I second that." Sarah wandered over to a table by the door. Three small pantry-like units sat against the wall on top of the table. She opened the first one with her teeth as her hands were still cuffed.

"Ouch," she said. "Look at this."

Adult toys in their original containers were piled one on top of the other. They all appeared to be butt plugs mixed in with an assortment of anal toys. She gestured at the largest one with a base as wide as a small Frisbee.

"Who could ever use that?"

Diner came over to stand beside her and opened the second door. Nipple clamps spilled out. More adult toys were stuffed inside. Everything from vibrating nipple clamps and rings for the base of the penis to ball stretchers and vaginal pumps.

The last door held vibrators, dildos, and a variety of devices that were supposed to be entered into the human body but appeared to be made for giants.

"Sarah, look," Diner said. "This is too large. How can they name it The Great American Challenge? The tip of this thing is the size of a baby's head. Who in their right mind would put this thing inside them?"

"What about that one?" Sarah nodded toward another item. "The Rambone. There's no way. Just no way."

Diner shut the door to the pantry unit. "We both know these aren't used willingly."

"I think now is a good time to use your phone. Call this place in. Let's shut it down."

Diner pulled out her phone, dialed a number, and held it to her ear.

Vivian whispered in Sarah's head.

The news was a letdown. A total loss of hope swept over Sarah even as Diner pulled her phone away and tried to dial again.

"It's no use," Sarah said.

"But I have to try."

"Signal jammers."

"What?"

"I was just informed that your phone won't work in this building."

"What? Why not? It has to work. We have to get out of here."

Sarah moved over to the chair in the corner and sat down, her bladder not happy she was sitting. "Not sure that's going to happen too soon."

"But Sarah, you brought us in here. You said bring your phone—"

"I also said I don't know everything!" she snapped. "Vivian tells me what I need to know when I need to know it."

"Well, right about now is a good time for her to tell you something useful, isn't it?"

Sarah stared at the tables covered in unique tools and wondered why they were inside the warehouse. What was the purpose?

Then Vivian started whispering. She explained what was important about medical room number two and why they were there as the door clicked open, and a crew of six men entered the room, Mr. Turner leading the way.

"Detective Marina Diner," Turner said. "You have disappointed us."

The guards behind him swung their weapons around and aimed them at her.

Turner smacked the cell phone out of Diner's hand. When Diner bent to pick it up, he raised his booted foot and came down on the back of her hand.

Diner screamed as bones crunched.

Turner ground his foot as if he was extinguishing a cigarette with his heel as Diner screamed louder.

Sarah's every urge was to attack Turner, hands cuffed behind her back or not. But she couldn't, as one of the machine guns was jammed in her neck, making any movement a gamble.

Finally, mercifully, Diner yanked her mangled hand out from under the boot and crawled away, holding her hand up.

"We know what happened at the funeral home." Turner spun to face Sarah. He stepped closer to her. "We know what you've been up to. And we were more than happy to allow you access to this room. Although I was surprised you chose this room."

"Why, because it leads to the panic room?" Sarah said.

"You know more than you should, but that's not the reason."

"Oh, right, because this is the room I kill you in."

He offered that brief smile again. "Cute. No, I was surprised because this was the room we sectioned off for your torture session once we picked you up off the street. Providing we got to you before the police did." He turned to face Diner. "But this female pig brought you to our doorstep, so the torture club is in session, and yours will begin as soon as Detective Diner has been dealt with."

The revulsion in her gut made her want to vomit on the man standing in front of her, but she managed to swallow it down.

"Dealt with?" Sarah asked. "Really? A bit weak, though, no? Unoriginal? Don't you mean raped and then killed, or cremated, or tortured?"

"Sarah Roberts, the violence I'll use to rend your limbs will be much worse than what happens to Marina here. But first, you get to watch Diner's end. Then you will be next."

Turner set his weapon on the far counter and turned to his men.

"Pick up the detective and get her on the table." He grabbed a circular saw from a section of drawers that opened to various tools. "Let's have some fun."

He turned on the saw.

Chapter 31

THE THUNDER OF GUNFIRE erupted from somewhere in the building. It was so loud and long that it could be heard over the racket of the circular saw.

Turner cocked an ear and listened momentarily as three men struggled with Diner to get her on the table.

Sarah didn't care what was happening outside the room at the moment. She studied the men in the room, looking for weaknesses, someone she could attack, limited as she was with her hands cuffed behind her back.

They got Diner up. Her arms splayed, the sound of the plastic crinkling under her body. The man holding her wounded hand squeezed the injury, a look of absolute joy on his face as Diner yelled, her eyes fluttering on the verge of passing out.

"Don't," Sarah shouted. "Don't you dare pass out on me, woman."

The saw shut down. Turner let it fall to the side of his leg.

"And why not?" he asked. "What does it matter? She has maybe ten minutes to live. Aren't you merciful?"

"I want her to be awake when you die. I want her to see what's coming."

A shadow crossed his eyes as if doubt had crept up and rooted a new spot in his thoughts. Or maybe it was fear. She would've missed it if she hadn't been staring straight at him.

Gunfire erupted outside the door in another part of the warehouse again. Something was going on, and she could tell Turner wondered if it had anything to do with them.

"You two," he motioned to the men by the door. "Go see what's going on."

They did an about-face and were gone, the door closing behind them rapidly.

"Friends of yours out there?" Turner asked. "They won't make it out of the building." He turned back to Diner, who seemed to have lost her struggle. She lay on the table, panting softly, eyes closed. The men attending to her held on tight, almost in fear that at any moment, she would spring up from her position on the table. "Regardless of what is happening out there," he added, "we continue in here."

He started up the saw again. Diner renewed her struggle, kicking and screaming.

"Hold her!" he yelled over the noise of the saw.

No one watched Sarah. She wondered if it was because she was cuffed and deemed non-threatening. But what did matter was getting that saw out of his hands, and without the use of her own hands, she was severely limited.

Turner brought the saw up and focused on Diner's lower

leg. He would begin to cut in seconds, and if the detective survived this ordeal, she would be maimed for the rest of her life.

Sarah jumped up, took two large steps, and dove head-first at Turner. He had been expecting her. Before she made contact, he swung the saw around toward her approach. When she dove, she came in low. Before making contact with his body, the horrid vibration of the saw and its blade hit her upper back.

A right shoulder might pack some weight on a football field, but down here, hands secured behind her as she body-checked his thigh, all that happened was Sarah bounced off his thick body and rolled painfully into the corner.

A sharp agony rose near her shoulder blade like a colony of a thousand bees stung her in the same spot. Her bladder released mercifully, wetting her pants thoroughly. Through gritted teeth, she screamed while Turner flicked off the saw to laugh.

Sarah cried out as blood slid down her spine and pooled around her buttocks. She wondered how bad the injury was, how deep it went. How much blood could she lose before she passed out?

Diner yelled over Turner's laughter, but Sarah couldn't hear it. Something about her being okay.

Then the door burst open. The two men from before ran back in, their guns no longer slung over their shoulders but held firmly in their hands.

Turner set the saw down on the table between Diner's ankles.

"Sir, we're under attack," one of the men reported. "They've breached the outer perimeter."

Turner wiped the sweat from around his mouth and asked, "Who?"

"Looks like ETF, sir."

"Where are the girls?"

"Being rounded up for the cage."

"How much time?"

"Minutes, sir. Maybe less."

When he turned to Sarah, the look of hatred in his eyes made her stare back at him, trying to evaluate his next move.

"Bring them in," he said without looking away from Sarah. "Do it now."

"Yes, sir."

The men disappeared, leaving the door wide open as Turner pulled the saw from the table and set it on the floor. Then he shoved the table across the room with Diner still on it. When it hit the far wall, Diner smacked into it, bounced back, and fell off the table, smacking the tiled floor hard.

The pain in Sarah's shoulder continued to rise like a tsunami of needles poking around her flesh. She squeezed her hands. All fingers responded. She flexed her biceps, then triceps. Everything worked as it should.

Maybe it was just a flesh wound. But it hurt like a bitch.

She looked down at her feet and followed the saw's cord to the wall where it was plugged in. Turner was working on something in the floor, spinning a dial that was just under the edge of the tile. She knew he was accessing the panic room. She had to stop anyone from entering, or they would never get out. It could only be opened once—the way Turner was opening it. As a safeguard, the code changed each time it was opened, and the other two that knew how to work it was dead.

She leaned forward and picked up the circular saw's cord with her foot as the men who had been holding Diner fled the room. With Diner writhing on the floor, her broken hand held high, and Sarah bleeding and handcuffed, they no longer posed any kind of threat.

Sarah managed to get the saw's cord wrapped around her right ankle three times.

As the noise of machine-gun fire continued outside the open door, she turned to her side and got onto her knees. Without looking back at Turner, she used her good shoulder against the cupboards to push off and get to her feet. The smell in her shirt from the Chinese restaurant had grown fainter, replaced by the smell of her urine with a touch of copper from the blood.

Turner had opened something. He grabbed a large handle and twisted it, then walked five feet to his right and twisted another handle.

Like the kind found on old farmhouses, a door opened out of the floor.

Guards and girls began to fill the room. As Sarah and Diner watched, Turner ushered them down the stairs to the floor. Naked woman after naked woman took to the stairs. One woman, missing her arm below the elbow, wobbled on her way down. Another woman with no hands walked by. Two men followed, and then Sarah's eyes welled up with tears when she saw a woman with both her eyes removed, being guided by two others, girls who didn't look a day out of high school. What looked like white golf balls had been placed in her empty sockets. A parade of at least a dozen other women in various states of undress entered the gaping hole in the medical room's floor, helped down by Turner and his cohorts.

Sarah looked at Diner, who had quieted in the corner. Their eyes met, and Sarah saw the pain and terror at what she was witnessing.

Then Turner moved around the people entering the panic room in the basement and came for Sarah.

She had been waiting for him. She had to forget the pain and ignore it to stay alive. She had done it before, and she could do it again. The shoulder wound would heal, but favoring it would kill her.

With the circular saw's cord wrapped firmly around her ankle, she pivoted in a circle like a shot putter preparing for a throw, her leg spinning out and wide, bringing the saw with her.

Turner saw the device coming and managed to jump over it the first time, but the second time it clunked into the back of his leg, barely nudging his bulk. The saw dropped to the floor, useless.

"Is that all you've got?" he shouted at her.

Sarah nodded, then shrugged. "I guess that's it."

Without thinking or wondering how effective it would be, fueled by the anger of all the pain and abuse that had taken place in this warehouse, Sarah lunged at him again, diving higher this time. At the moment before contact, she spun in a circle so his grabbing hands would have difficulty finding purchase.

She caught him slightly off balance. When he took a step back to right himself, he tripped over the saw and teetered backward, his arms pinwheeling for balance.

Sarah dropped to the floor beside the open door to the panic room and spun around as Turner fell backward into the hole where all the captives had just descended. He landed at the bottom of the stairs with a clunk and a short moan of pain.

The man at the door brought his gun to bear on Sarah and stepped closer.

"Enough of your meddling," he said.

A canister spewing gas rolled in between the man's legs. Then pockets of blood opened up in his vest. He blinked and looked down. Blood pulsed out of the new holes in his chest.

"Hey," he said. "What the—"

He fell beside her as Sarah began to cough, her eyes welling up from the effects of the gas. Another man fell, blood coming from a neck wound.

The large door to the panic room was closing. How many people had made it in there while she got the saw wrapped around her ankle and fought with Turner? Twenty, thirty?

In a last-ditch effort, Sarah swung her foot—the saw's cord still attached to it—around hard. The saw followed and came to rest beside the opening to the panic room. Just as the door was about to drop firmly closed, she nudged the thick saw in place, and the door stopped, the engine controlling its movement, grinding gears. It ground for another few seconds, then quieted.

With her hands still behind her back, Sarah couldn't wipe her eyes, but whatever the gas was, it made her sneeze and cough again.

"Clear," someone yelled, their voice muffled by a mask.

Men wearing helmets, goggles, breathing apparatus, and Kevlar jackets with POLICE stenciled on their backs entered medical room number two.

"Two down," one of them yelled. "Need medics in here

now. Got a bleeder, too."

Then five of them forced the panic room door open and charged down the stairs.

Sarah could barely see through the tears clogging her eyes, but she knew it was over. The girls could go home now.

Sarah curled up by the cupboards to hide her face from the gas still coming out of the canister.

This time Vivian was right. It was better she didn't have the whole picture until now. She would've died coming in here with a machine gun, blasting away at men like Turner.

This was the only way. It had to be handled like this.

But it's not over, Sarah.

She was reminded of the black book and the man Marshall Machiavelli answered to. She knew that this man was on the run. He was heading to one of his other torture clubs in Amsterdam to lock it down and wait out the heat.

Vivian said she'd tell her what she needed to know soon.

But first, get to the Toronto airport by morning and buy a ticket for Amsterdam on a KLM flight leaving at noon.

Diner dropped beside her, interrupting her thoughts. Sarah looked up through tears as Diner set a mask over her nose.

"You okay?" Diner asked.

Sarah nodded. "It's just so sad. I've seen a lot in my life, but this is …"

Diner shook her head. "I know."

Together they watched as girl after girl was brought up from the panic room. Even as the paramedics arrived to deal with their wounds, Sarah and the detective waited until all the women left the basement before leaving medical room number two.

It was to honor them, to stand for them. To show the women someone still cared.

"It's over," Diner said.

"I'm afraid not," Sarah mumbled from behind her mask. "This is just the beginning."

Chapter 32

AN HOUR LATER, OUTSIDE in the parking lot, where the air was clean, and the tear gas symptoms had faded, Aaron came over and hugged her gently. When he pulled back, his nose was twitching.

"Don't ask," she said.

"Interesting." Aaron stepped back, eyebrows raised.

"That's all you're allowed to say about odors." She raised a finger. He nodded. "Now, how did you manage to pull this off?"

"Just as you directed in the note. Once Detective Diner left the apartment, Parkman called in a few favors. When we had the ear of a few high-ranking officials, the ones Vivian made you write down as safe and not in league with this place," he motioned at the warehouse, "the ETF were called in, and here we are."

"But they have sentries posted up and down the street."

"ETF took them out one by one, but as instructed, they waited until Detective Diner's car, with you two in it, entered the premises."

Diner was shaking her head. "I would've never believed it."

"Believed what?" Sarah asked.

"Even the pants." Diner looked away.

In the note, Sarah had asked Aaron to bring a change of pants. She had gladly discarded her blood and urine-soaked pants in the warehouse's restroom and now wore dry jeans, her Passport in the back pocket.

Medical personnel and police officers meandered throughout the parking lot dealing with the wounded. So far, they had rounded up twenty-five women. Eighteen needed hospital care, nine were maimed for life, and four girls would never walk again. Two girls had gone blind, and one woman found in a dark part of the warehouse had been subjected to acid over time, her skin burned and mottled beyond recognition. Seven women, too ill to run, had been murdered during the raid by guards as they fled the ETF's assault.

Diner gazed at Sarah. "This. My brother. All of it."

"Brother?" Aaron asked.

"Another story," Sarah said without looking away from Diner. "Now what?" she asked.

Sarah's cuffs had been removed, and paramedics had tended to her back wound. The saw's teeth had nicked the shoulder blade, the skin broken. They wanted to take her to get stitches, but she refused until the warehouse had been emptied of women, so they bandaged and dressed the wound the best they could.

Diner's hand had been tended to, but she was supposed

to head to the hospital for an X-ray, which she also refused for the time being.

"I was a full-fledged atheist before this. You aren't omnipresent. So how could you know what you knew without help?"

"It's one thing to hear about Vivian. It's another to see what she can do through me."

Diner nodded and looked down at her wounded hand. They stood side by side in silence, watching the authorities do their jobs. Diner was going to get the credit for the bust. A forensics team was at the funeral home taking pictures and logging the evidence. The paperwork would take weeks, but Sarah needed to know where Diner stood with everything Sarah had done.

"Can you see why I did what I did?" Sarah asked.

Diner nodded without hesitation.

"You watched the video on the CN Tower. Vanessa was about to fall. There was no way back. A suicide would not have ended this. No one would investigate. Her father, who fed this place with girls, wouldn't have been incensed. It was the only way."

"I know that now."

"Joel and Belinda had to die. The system wouldn't—"

"I was there," Diner cut in. "I saw the bodies. I would've had a hard time not killing them myself."

Sarah studied the detective's face. This could go either way. There was no more running. Either they would arrest her, and she'd be stuck in the system for years, or she would be on that plane tomorrow headed to Amsterdam.

"Do you remember me asking about Hitler and whether you would have killed him?"

"I remember."

"That's Fletcher's father in this picture. He sired Fletcher and Joel. He beat his wife until she died. He hated women. Then he joined the Torture Garden, the legal one that still operates worldwide today, and decided to create this place. The old man was dying in the hospital anyway, but being given a one-way ticket out of here—by a woman, no less— was pure hell for him." She had worked herself up, rousting new pain from her wound. Even her cheek, where the baseball bat had jabbed her, started hurting again.

"Look, Sarah, I have a lot of reports to write." Diner pushed off the cruiser she was leaning against. She stepped away, then stopped and turned back. "You're free to go."

"Go? How's that? I'm the most wanted woman in Toronto. And what about my statement? Aren't you going to need one?"

"Leave. Get to the airport. Do your thing. Don't worry about the paperwork. That's my job. I'll write it up without you here. The gun misfired on the CN Tower. It was an accident. Joel and Belinda were self-defense. Fletcher's dad asked for water and toilet paper to wipe his nose. How the hell could you have known he'd eat it? Niles Mason shot Timothy Simmons and tried to frame you. Then he shot two Toronto councilmen and committed suicide. If anything, you're the victim here. You were the unlucky one in all of this." She stepped back in front of Sarah. "After what I witnessed you do here, all these girls saved, at the expense of possibly losing your own life, there is no way I could repay you." Sarah's eyes watered at the mention of the damaged women. "Go get that bastard. Go get that black book. But I have one condition. Once you get that book, I get it. I want every single person who's involved with this warehouse to pay for what they have done. I won't rest until that day comes. Do we have a deal?"

"We do. But I need something from you."

Diner leaned back. "What I just said isn't enough?"

"It's not enough."

Aaron shrugged. Parkman was making his way over. Sarah waited for him to join them.

"What is it, Sarah?" Diner asked. "What do you want?"

"For your APBs or BOLOs to be updated before I leave here." She smiled, showing teeth. "If we leave and I get to the airport where I'm stopped and detained, it wouldn't be good."

"I've already sent out the word that we got you, and half an hour ago, I relayed the message to my superiors that you were innocent of everything and leaving Canada. No one will detain you."

"Great. Then that's it then."

"No, there's one more thing." Diner grabbed Sarah's arm with her good hand, nudged her closer, and hugged her, mindful of her back wound. "Thank you for reintroducing me to my brother," she whispered in Sarah's ear. "You have done more good than you will ever know." Diner was crying. Her body hitched with the tears slightly. "I will always remember you." She pulled back. "Sarah, woman to woman, I love you for what you have done here. Come back anytime. Stay with me. I'll make dinner. I owe you. Just leave your guns at home." She hiccupped a laugh through her tears.

Sarah wiped at her face. "I'll take you up on that."

They hugged again.

When Diner let go, she turned around and headed for the

open door of an ambulance. The doors closed, the ambulance pulled away, and Detective Marina Diner was gone.

"Parkman, Aaron, take me to the airport. Then we need a hotel, and I need a stiff drink." They started walking. "I need a bottle of whiskey. I don't want to feel anything for the next twelve hours."

"I know just the place," Parkman said.

In the car, heading toward the airport, Vivian whispered a daunting message to Sarah. *Tomorrow's plane will take off on time. It will have the man she's hunting. It will be headed to Amsterdam as planned.*

But there will be an incident that leads it to crash, and there's nothing she can do about it. There will be survivors, but innocents might be killed, too.

Will my target be on the plane? Sarah asked for clarity.

Yes ...

Sarah stared at the passing high-rise buildings of Toronto as Parkman drove to the airport. Aaron sat beside her, his hand in hers. They would talk tonight. They would mend fences. They would make shelves.

And tomorrow, she would get on that plane whether it went down or not because that was who she was. No one understood her like Vivian. Not even Aaron.

That was why she wouldn't tell him that the plane would crash.

Her target was getting on that plane. Because of that, nothing would stop her from boarding it, too.

Nothing.

Because sometimes there were more important things in life than worrying about death. Sometimes some things were greater than us. And even in the face of *death*, how could she *live* with herself if she didn't go after her target?

Locating the black book would reveal the names of the criminals as well as the victims. Finding her target and stopping him from masterminding more torture clubs would free the torture of the future.

Those girls who walked out of medical room number two had been abandoned and lost. But now they were free.

She would get on that plane for The Abandoned ones around the world.

Fear was an illusion. It was one she couldn't afford.

The price of fear was too high.

Too damn high.

Afterword

(*Spoiler Alert! Read *after* you've read the novel.)

I've always wanted to explore that question of what I would do when Hitler was named Time's Man of the Year in 1938 if I knew what I know now. As a writer, I get that opportunity.

In performing her tasks in Toronto, I also wanted to have Sarah irrevocably appear to be a murderer. I wanted YouTube videos, actual footage of Sarah Roberts pulling the trigger and killing someone. Once that was done, killing Joel and Belinda was icing on the cake.

Enter the strait-laced detective who never breaks the rules, and you've got Sarah in a lot of trouble.

Writing myself into a box, as I like to call it, is a favorite pastime of mine. The first time I ever wrote myself into a box was in *The Warning*, book two, when Sarah was locked inside a small portable jail on a commune near an abandoned airplane hangar. The room was square. A hole was cut in the floor as a toilet, and the only way in and out was through the door, but that was padlocked and chained closed. There was virtually no way out.

I spent almost two weeks at my desk trying to get her out of that jail. I finally had her burrow under the hole in the toilet and crawl on the feces-encrusted dirt to the far wall, where she was shot twice—grazed—and then finally escaped.

Writing myself into a corner is too much fun for me. And that was my goal for this novel.

Why do I use Toronto as a location so often?

I spent many years in Toronto, and no matter where I travel throughout the world, Toronto has a special place in my heart. In the mid-eighties, I bought cassettes at Sam The Record Man on Yonge Street. I went to the Amnesty International concert in 1987 at Maple Leaf Gardens and saw Bruce Springsteen and Peter Gabriel, among others. That concert went on so long that night we couldn't get a train out of the city. My friend and I spent the night walking the streets of downtown Toronto until the first train out of Union Station the next morning. We fell asleep in the lobby of the Royal York Hotel—featured in book seven, *The Vigilante*, although it was called the Royal Oak Hotel, and it's also featured in book thirty-two, *The Game*—then got kicked out by security. And we bought coffee, one after another, at an all-night restaurant until the sun rose and the trains began rolling again.

I remember AC/DC's "Who Made Who" concert at the

CNE Fairgrounds in the summer of 1986. It was so intense that when the trains pulled up to take people out of the area, there was a riot. Concertgoers attacked the GO Train (Government of Ontario Train) and destroyed them. GO canceled any other trains, and everyone had to find their own way home. We ended up using a taxi service, which was pricey in those days on a high school budget.

I know not all the memories of Toronto are good, but they are memories that became stories around the campfire. Like when I was swarmed by seven other guys in a Radio Shack in the mall and sucker punched in the face because I looked at a guy wrong. Insane stuff, but man, that's not even the worst of it. I've got dozens of true stories, near misses, and absolute insanity on the streets of Toronto that ultimately led me to raise my daughters outside its borders.

But I also have a bevy of fond memories, and when I can, I like to go back to Toronto, to my old haunts, and walk down memory lane, hence the use of Toronto as a location numerous times in my novels. I've been to many places I write about, like The Office. A bunch of friends and I would always meet there on Tuesday nights back in the early '90s for Wing Night. I miss those days.

But alas, we must all grow up and move on. At least I can walk those streets, relive those memories, and enjoy Toronto through Sarah's eyes. Not the violent parts, though. I'll let Sarah deal with that shit.

When I turned eighteen, I joined a Canadian Protection Services company as a security guard. I worked my way up to Patrol Supervisor and eventually attained my Private Investigator License several years later. When Jamie Stratton —the Eaton's Centre security guard in this novel—found the white Dodge Charger and dropped to the ground in an attempt to secure the plate number of the car unseen, you were reading a true story. I did that exact thing when I was younger. I still recall the plate number that got a sex offender arrested and put behind bars. He didn't see me—he never saw me coming.

Just like Jamie Stratton, I applied to Durham Regional Police to be a cop, but I failed the spelling test. I know, I can't believe it either!

I'll stop there and say that these novels are not anything remotely close to being a memoir. This is entirely fiction with a little of the "write what you know" mixed in.

Many people help with each novel, and I want to thank them here.

My editor, Robb Grindstaff—also an amazing writer—I couldn't do it without him. We're in our fourth year of working together, and I can't express how valuable he is to me.

So, to my editor, I thank you.

My daughters, Bethany and Odette, whom I love dearly. The next book, *The Abandoned*, is on its way, but in its early stages, my daughter Odette came up with a plot line I couldn't resist. Watch for *The Abandoned*'s release, and when it comes out, and you've read it, the Afterword will explain her role. Bethany has offered numerous points that I've had to fix and even does last-minute edits for me. She's becoming quite the writer herself.

Lastly, the readers. I could not do this without you. You are my heroes. I love you all. That is why in *The Enigma*, Sarah Roberts book six, I had a cop named Mara as a dedication to Mara Martinez. I have used other friends' and readers' names in the past and the names of people I don't particularly like.

In this novel, the Turner brothers were used lightly. Turner was the name of a boy from grade two that took a chip out of my front tooth when he jammed my face into the tiled floor of the school hallway. Ever since that single act of stupidity, I have spent years in and out of dentist offices fixing my front teeth. They remained fragile since the first time they were fixed. A hockey puck in the mouth broke it once. A misjudged beer bottle smacked it out. A considerably sticky piece of Halloween toffee pulled the broken piece loose again. Back to the dentist over and over. The last time it was fixed was in 2011. It hasn't broken since, and I hope it stays in place for a while longer.

In *The Haunted*, book twelve, I used Sandra Gonzales's name. Sandra is a wonderful human being, and I'm so grateful to have her as a reader.

I used Marina Diner as my detective in this book, *The Unlucky*. Marina is a real person whom I am also so grateful to have as a reader. I appreciate her enthusiasm when a new novel comes out. I don't know these people personally, but as readers, I love them.

And Gigi, I hope you saw that you were the waitress in The Office Pub on John Street.

Thank you for reading, and I hope you join Sarah's ride for many more novels to come.

The Abandoned, book fourteen, is on its way when Sarah heads to Amsterdam and ends up in Greece.

Then book fifteen deals with a drug cartel, one Sarah has unwittingly pissed off.

And there's so much more coming.

Get caught reading …
Jonas Saul

About Jonas Saul

Jonas Saul is the bestselling author of the Sarah Roberts Series—more than two million sold!—and has written and published over sixty thrillers. After acquiring an agent, he signed several deals in Los Angeles, with MadRiver Pictures optioning his Sarah Roberts Series—over forty books!—(currently in development).

Jonas has often outranked Stephen King and Dean

Koontz on Amazon over the past decade. He's regularly invited to be a guest speaker, teacher, or workshop presenter at international writing conferences and film festivals worldwide. He hosts an annual writer's retreat in Greece, where he currently lives. He focuses his teaching on how to get tension and emotion in every scene, on every page, how he made it as a creator/writer, the path to success in this business, and the pitfalls to avoid. He also hosts a reading retreat in Greece with guest authors, yoga retreats, and hiking retreats. Visit the Imagine Greece Retreats website at www.imaginegreeceretreats.com, or email him directly to discuss an opportunity to join one of the retreats at jonas@imaginegreeceretreats.com.

Jonas is also a professional freelance editor. He works for several publishers and does private editing for clients, with many testimonials on his website at www.imaginepress.org, which details each author's response to Jonas's editing skills. Email Jonas directly for an editing quote at editor@imaginepress.org.

To book Jonas for a speaking engagement at a writer's conference/festival, to have him on your jury at a film festival, or even to say hello, email Jonas directly at jonassaul@icloud.com.

For updates on releases, hit the "Follow" button on Amazon or Bookbub, and join Jonas on Facebook, where he's most active.

Contact Jonas Saul

Linktree: Find me here

Email: jonassaul@icloud.com

9 781998 047352